A BABY FOR FLORENCE

BOOK 9 THE AMISH BONNET SISTERS

SAMANTHA PRICE

D1522502

FLORENCE LOVED every season in the apple orchard. Each one brought its own special delights, but she couldn't deny that the spring blossoms with their varying shades of pink were the most beautiful sight of all. The air carried the sweet fragrance of the blooms as well as the scents of new life, rebirth, and the hope of all kinds of possibilities.

The bees buzzed by, busy doing their most necessary of jobs, and the birds were happily tweeting and flying about. The robins were another welcome sight that marked the beginning of Spring. They were delightful except when they were making a feast of the young apples. This morning, a robin had sat on their kitchen windowsill chirping as she and Carter drank their morning coffee. It was a pleasant start to their day.

As she took Spot on his walk, Florence glanced at

the Bakers' orchard. Their mature apple trees were beautiful, and it would take years for hers to compare. Right now, her orchard-to-be was level ground with no sign of vegetation. The extensive drainage had been finished, so they'd come a long way in the last couple of months. It would take her a long time, though, to replace what had been stolen from her. That was how it had felt, but she'd decided to let go of those feelings of resentment a long time ago.

It had been her decision to leave her home and her Amish family to marry Carter. She left knowing she would be cut off from her family and her father's orchard. It didn't matter that she'd known that. It still hurt. Her heart ached every time she thought about her father's orchard being in another man's hands. Not just any man, one who had always disliked her for no good reason. Levi Bruner had married her stepmother and had stepped into her shoes as keeper of the orchard even though he knew less than nothing about looking after trees.

It hurt even more when she learned he intended using non-organic chemicals, in and around the trees, when her orchard had always been organic. If he proceeded along those lines, and she prayed every night that he wouldn't, then her own orchard would have little chance of being organic accredited since the chemicals would leach into the ground and drift on the winds.

The only hope of her getting back her family's

orchard was for Levi to run it into the ground and then she'd buy it from them. The thought of that, though, brought her little joy. By then, the orchard would be destroyed, and her stepmother Wilma would be devastated. Florence didn't want that to happen.

Florence leaned against the fencepost and stared at her beloved trees. Her father would've had no idea what would happen. Since her two older brothers had never been interested in the orchard, he'd taught Florence everything as though she'd be the one to take it over. For that reason alone, she felt guilty for leaving. If she'd stayed, would Wilma have ever married Levi? Levi had chased Wilma and showed his interest, but *Mamm* had never shown much interest in return until Florence left. Then they surprised everyone by announcing their wedding.

Mamm had never been strong, either mentally or physically and needed someone to rely upon. That person was now Levi. And now Levi was responsible for the three unmarried girls still living at home. He also brought with him his own daughter, Bliss, who was around the same age as Hope.

Spot pulled on his lead. He was ready to keep walking. She walked on.

The baby growing inside her was her chance at a new life and a new beginning. She'd take everything her father taught her about apples and use it to full advantage with the orchard she and Carter were growing from scratch.

Now the weather was warm enough to fertilize the trees in the Baker orchard, and prune where needed.

But the question was, was Levi aware of that?

Trees were like people and each needed to be treated as an individual, but what would Levi know about that?

Nothing, and neither would he care, she feared.

All she could do was pray that he'd have a change of heart. For a stubborn man like Levi, that would require a true miracle, like the parting of the Red Sea, or the manna falling from heaven.

Two starlings swooped overhead, and then darted about her and the dog. Spot took a leap at them, jerking on the lead. "No, Spot."

Spot pulled on the lead again when they landed on the fence close by, seeming to taunt him. He clearly wanted to give chase.

"Stop it!"

That was why she always had to keep him on a lead outside. He'd most likely catch one of them and then Florence didn't know what she'd do. When he pulled on the lead for a third time, this time jolting her whole body, it was time to end the walk.

"Back to the house, Spot." He knew what those words meant. As they ambled home, Florence scolded him. "If you can't behave, I'll leave you home when I go for a walk. How would you like that?" He looked up at her with his soft brown eyes. She was sure he knew every word she was saying. "Just behave, okay? Then we won't have a problem."

CHERISH BAKER WAS WORKING on the northern side of the Bakers' Apple Orchard along with her stepfather Levi and her new stepsister, Bliss. She was tolerating them the best she could. Levi was making an effort to fit in with the family and she liked Levi a little more because of it. He now saw sense in keeping the apple orchard running how it had always been, an organic orchard offering organic apples. That was what their customers expected and if they didn't produce those, they'd be competing with cheaper imported goods. It made sense to keep things as they were. It was when Levi came across a book in a library that he'd had the change of heart. Now he had bought a copy and was following most of what it said.

He was even using her father's old recipe to oil the trees. It was something her father had done early every Spring. It helped to keep away pests and he'd had his own secret recipe to make it. Cherish was showing them how to apply it. She'd done it so many times as a young girl tagging behind Florence and asking questions. Back then she wasn't really that interested, and neither was she now. Everything in her life held little excitement. She was just filling in time before she went back to the farm that Aunt Dagmar had left her. That was where she felt truly alive. Her plan was, as soon as she was old enough, she'd leave home for good.

As Bliss painted some oil on a tree, she turned to Cherish and said, "Did you know it's my birthday soon?"

"*Jah*, you told everyone at the breakfast table this morning, and at dinner last night."

"Oh, did I?" Bliss giggled. "I don't want a fuss made."

"Good." Cherish went back to thinking about the farm. Nothing would give her more pleasure than to give her farm's caretaker his marching orders. Malachi had a mind of his own and wasn't one to take instructions well. She'd told him she wanted nothing changed and every time she visited, he'd made changes.

"I would like a dog, though," Bliss said.

Cherish stood up with brush still in hand. "A dog?" She was talking about her birthday—again. "*Mamm* would never allow another dog. Caramel and Goldie drive her to insanity as it is."

"A cat, then."

"*Nee*, never. The barn cats would fight with it. They're cranky old things."

"I'll keep him in the *haus* with me."

"*Nee*. The dogs mostly live in the *haus* and they'd eat him. Well, Caramel lives in the *haus* now that Goldie stays in the caravan with Joy and Isaac."

Bliss blew out a deep breath and Cherish almost felt sorry for her.

"Don't we have enough animals about the place for you to play with?"

"*Jah* we do. *You've* got a dog *and* a bird."

"What if I give you Timmy?"

Bliss shook her head. "He only goes to you. He won't even jump onto my hand."

"That's true. You came into this family late and all the pet spaces were taken up."

"*Jah,* Bliss. You don't need an animal. It's another mouth to feed and we have enough of those."

Cherish stared over at her stepfather. It was a typical comment that he would make. He was so focused on money above all else. Penny pinching is what he did. It was because of him that the apples had rotted on the trees last season. Someone other than the family members must've told him he'd likely make more money keeping the orchard organic. That was something he wouldn't have figured out by himself.

Once Cherish noticed Bliss's mouth turn down at the corners and her cheeks puff out, she decided then and there to get her stepsister *some* kind of pet for her birthday. One that would fit in with the animals they already had. She'd give it a lot of thought. There must be some variety of creature that *Mamm* wouldn't object to that would get along with the barn cats and the dogs. On second thought, nothing got along with the barn cats. The new pet would have to be kept away from those.

"I just won't have a birthday at all then," Bliss announced as she went back to painting the branches.

"Gut. I'll tell *Mamm* not to bake your favorite German Cherry Cake," Levi had a spark of amusement in his voice, a sound Cherish hadn't heard from him before.

"Nee, please, don't tell *Mamm* that. That's her favorite and mine too." That set Bliss off into peals of high-pitched giggles.

Cherish crinkled her nose. The only thing that annoyed Cherish more than Bliss's giggles was when Bliss called her mother *Mamm.* She wasn't her *mudder,* she was her stepmother. Calling her that might've been okay if she had been raised by *Mamm* from a two-year-old as was Florence, but Bliss was nearly a grown woman with a full memory of her own mother. Not only was it disrespectful to Bliss's late mother, it was weird. It would be better to call her Wilma and be done with it. Or even Aunt Wilma, to show she was more than a friend.

Cherish set about working to pass the time. Only a couple more years and then she could leave this place and all the annoying people who inhabited it. Then she'd live a good life—one where she could make all her own decisions.

CHAPTER 2

"I'M TELLING MY PARENTS TONIGHT," Fairfax announced to Hope Baker.

"Telling them what?" Hope wanted him to say he was telling them about her. That the two of them were in love. It wasn't easy loving an *Englisher*. He had to join them if they were to be together, because she was never going to leave her Amish community. He knew it.

"I'm telling them I'm going to see your bishop about joining."

Hope stared at Fairfax. "You've been saying you'll speak to the bishop for weeks and you haven't done it. Why do you need to talk to your parents about it?" That was the first time he'd mentioned talking to them. In her opinion, he was too old to need their approval.

"It's just that I want them to know what I'm doing."

"Is that the reason, or are you hoping they'll talk you out of it?" Hope crossed her arms tightly over her chest. He'd gotten her hopes up and she'd kept quiet, waiting for him to bring up the subject again. Talking to his parents was a delay tactic; she was certain of it. "Or do you need their approval? You're a grown man and besides that, aren't they leaving soon to retire in Florida? Isn't that why they sold their orchard to Florence and Carter?"

"That's right about them leaving soon. I don't need their approval at all. I can make up my own mind. Already have made up my mind. It's just that I respect them and want to keep them in the loop of what I'm doing."

As much as Hope loved him, she wouldn't wait for him forever. His indecision was causing her to wonder about him. Fairfax had told her he was going to speak with the bishop and that was what she wanted him to do. She needed him to be a man of his word. If he wasn't, it meant he wasn't the right man for her. What she needed was a man with principles that she respected. She couldn't respect him when he didn't do what he said.

"I'll talk to them tonight and—"

"And see the bishop when?"

"Soon."

What if they disapproved? Was he hoping they wouldn't approve, so he'd have an easy way out? "Do what you want, Fairfax. I don't want you to think I'm forcing you. It's got to be your own decision. If you regret telling me what you told me, take it back. But don't leave me hanging and waiting for something that's never going to happen."

"Fair enough. Would you leave the community for me?"

"No."

He glanced over at her. "You said that pretty quickly."

"I'm happy with my life. I don't want to change it, but neither do I want to lose you. The only way we can be together is if you join us. It's a huge decision for you. Your life will be very different, and you may not like it."

"It would be nice if you'd do anything for me, like leaving. That'll make me feel better about making the sacrifices."

"See you've got it all wrong. You're looking at what you'll be giving up rather than what you'll be gaining. You're not ready, Fairfax. Perhaps we shouldn't see each other for a while so you can really think this through."

He grunted, and his eyebrows moved together in a frown. "So, you don't want me to tell my folks tonight?"

"I want you to think about everything and it sounds like you're too undecided to tell anyone."

"That's it then? If I don't join, we're over?"

Why was this all so hard? "I never wanted to like you, it just happened. I didn't plan this. I don't know what to say."

The rest of the drive to Hope's home was spent in silence. Fairfax drove her to and from work every day, in secret from her parents, who thought she was riding her bike to the bed and breakfast for her cleaning job. All her sisters knew she was secretly dating Fairfax. Joy, one of her older sisters, told her no good would come of dating him and it looked like Joy was right. If Fairfax left her now, she'd be left with heartache and sorrow.

He stopped his pickup truck at the usual spot, not too far from her house. Without talking to her, he got out and pulled her bike off the bed of the truck.

"Thanks, Fairfax," she said as she took hold of the handlebars. Now she would ride up the driveway as though she'd ridden home.

"Where do we go from here?" He looked down at her.

She was lost for words. Was it better to end things now or have his indecision dragging on for years? "I don't know." She bit her lip. It was really up to him. He knew where she stood.

He inhaled deeply. "I've got a lot to think about." He placed his hand on her shoulder. "Don't think that I don't have really strong feelings for you, but I have a lot to consider. I'm sorry I told you I'd speak to your bishop. I said that before I really thought it through. I wanted to take our relationship to the next level and that was all I could see to do to get it there."

"I understand." She really didn't. What was he saying exactly?

"We'll take time apart and then see each other when I've had time to think. Is that okay with you?"

"Of course."

"Only thing is, I'm worried about you on your bike all that way to work and back six days a week."

She fixed a smile on her face. "Don't worry, the weather is warmer now. I might see if one of the girls can take me in the buggy. They're often going that way in the mornings and then I'll only have one trip to do."

"Okay. That makes me feel better. Bye, Hope." They stared into each other's eyes for a moment. She desperately wanted him to make up his mind then and there. All of a sudden, he leaned forward and planted a kiss on her cheek. Then he strode away, got in his vehicle, and sped off leaving her in a cloud of fine dust.

Hope stood there staring after him with her fingertips lingering where his lips had been. How had things gone downhill so fast? She'd had dreams of marrying him in an Amish wedding, him in white shirt, suspenders, bow tie, and black pants. If he never came back to her, she'd be left with the meager selection of men in their Amish community.

No one would ever compare.

She threw one leg over the bike and pedaled home trying to ignore the ache that felt like a gaping hole in her heart. Her Amish community was what stood between them. Was that a mountain too high for him to climb? Maybe she shouldn't have told him so many times that the bishop wouldn't want him to join for a girl. Without her, though, he would probably never dream of joining them. Was it so bad to join the community for love?

By the time Hope got to the bottom of the driveway, tears were trickling down her cheeks. She'd never felt so wretched. There was nothing she could do but wait on Fairfax's decision. If only he hadn't gotten her hopes up.

When she got to the barn to put the bike away, she heard some sounds and looked over into the back of the building. It was Joy raking out the stalls.

Joy looked up at her, dropped her pitchfork and ran to her. "What's happened?"

"Fairfax," she managed to say.

"Is he all right?"

She nodded. "I think we've just broken up."

Joy pulled her over to some hay bales and they sat and then Hope told her the whole story.

"You did the right thing," Joy told her as she rubbed her back.

"It doesn't feel right," Hope said between sobs.

"You'll get over him." Hope cried on Joy's shoulder and Joy put her arm around her. "Whatever happens was meant to be. Remember, all things work together for the good. He could join us, or he may not and then the love of your life might appear, and you won't think twice about Fairfax."

"My faith isn't as strong as yours is, Joy."

Joy rubbed Hope's arm. "You only need a tiny pinch

of faith. It's like seasoning in cooking. Just a pinch makes everything far better."

"I'll try to remember that, but I thought we'd be married, and things would be perfect. I never thought we'd be broken up and that's what this feels like."

"Give him time, Hope, and just know that any decision he makes is the right one for the both of you."

CHAPTER 3

WHEN JOY and Hope walked inside, they were faced with a frantic Bliss in the kitchen. Her cheeks were red and she was darting about pulling pots and pans out of the cupboard.

"What's going on?" asked Joy.

"*Mamm's* got a migraine, so she's in bed. I've got no idea where Cherish is. She seems to always disappear when I need her most. Favor's helping *Dat* in the orchard now, and I'm trying to bake for the mud sale."

Joy took a step backward. "Time I go back home." Home was the caravan that had been towed on site some weeks ago, so she and her new husband could have their own private space while saving for a home.

"What are you trying to bake?" asked Hope.

"Trying?"

"Um, I'm sorry. What are you baking?"

17

SAMANTHA PRICE

"A funnel cake. Three, actually. *Mamm* promised them for Ada."

"I forgot about the mud sale tomorrow. I'm working so I can't go. By the time I finish, it'll all be over. Do you want some help?"

"Would you, Hope?"

"Of course." Hope felt sorry for Bliss. It couldn't have been easy for her to fit in with the remaining four sisters that lived on the property. Everyone was adjusting to the new family dynamic. "I help *Mamm* every year with them. The funnel section needs to have an opening of 1/2 inch or so and hold about a cup of batter."

"I've got the batter ready." She held up a cup.

"*Gut*. Now add the cup of batter into the funnel and let it run slowly through in swirls and zigzags into the center of the oil."

"It seems so hard."

Hope smiled. "Everything seems like that the first time you do it." She watched Bliss do what she was told. "Now is when to do the criss-cross motion to make the design." Once that was done, Hope poked it with a fork to separate some of the layers. "Great. Now pop it into the oven and you need to check the bottom. When it's golden brown, flip it over so the other side will cook. You'll have to do it carefully, so it won't break."

"Got it."

"Then you take it out and let it drain."

"*Denke,* Hope. I think I can do it now."

"You're welcome." Hope looked around. "I guess I'll start on dinner."

"*Jah,* I've not started, and no one's been here to help me until you came. You'll have to cook something that doesn't need the oven."

"I can use the stovetop. I'll use some of the leftover meat from last night and we'll have a potato pie. Oh, wait, that'll need the oven."

"I'll be finished by the time you cook the potatoes."

Together the two girls worked in the kitchen. Bliss was pleased to have some company and Hope was pleased that she didn't have to think about what Fairfax was doing tonight. Was he talking things over with his parents, or was he putting things out of his mind completely?

Over dinner that night, Joy and Isaac joined them, and everyone was talking about the mud sale.

"Joy and I are going to see if we can get things for our new home in the auctions."

Cherish giggled at Isaac's comment. "How about you get the home first? Or do you mean the steel trap you're living in?"

Isaac wasn't offended. "Our new home. The one we're going to buy as soon as we can. We'll even have you over for dinner, Cherish, if you're nice to us."

"That'll never happen," Joy joked.

"I'll be nice to whoever can take me back to the farm."

"You and the farm, Cherish. You were only there in December. Don't you know it can carry on without you?" Favor said.

Timmy started chirping loudly.

"Cherish, cover the bird up," Levi snarled. "Your *mudder* won't want to hear that with her headache."

"Sure." Cherish got up and covered Timmy's cage. "Goodnight, Timmy." When she sat back down at the table, she said, "Timmy heard the farm mentioned. He's a smart bird. He probably misses home and Aunt Dagmar. I miss her too." She pushed her food around on her plate, then she looked up. "So, who's going to take me back there?"

"How can anyone take you back?" Isaac asked. "It's not as though we can drive a buggy all that way."

"I think it's her way of asking my permission if she can ask Florence and Carter to drive her there," Levi said.

"Well, can I?" Cherish peeped at Levi from under her lashes.

"I'll need your help in the orchard for the next two weeks and then you'll have to see if you can get time off from your job at the coffee shop." He shook his fork at her. "When you come back, I'll expect you to keep looking for a full-time job or just get more work where you are."

"*Denke*, Levi. But I have been working every day in the orchard, so isn't *that* full employment in a way?"

Cherish cringed. She knew she was going to get the same old tired answer.

"We need money now. We have bills to pay today. I know we'll get money at harvest time but that's months away."

"We're doing what we can to find work," Bliss said. "No one is hiring."

"They could always go back to having a roadside stall," Joy said. "We did that for years and made good money until harvest came."

"*Nee!*" And that was all that Levi said about the matter, and then he went back to eating.

Cherish and Joy exchanged looks. Each knew what the other was thinking. Levi was a stubborn man and they were stuck with him. Cherish had overheard *Mamm* talking to her best friend Ada, recently. Levi had apologized to Wilma when they'd had that argument before *Mamm* went up north to be with Mercy and Honor for the births of their first children. *Mamm* and Levi seemed to get along better, and after the overheard conversation Cherish knew why. If Cherish were in her mother's shoes, she'd never forgive him for calling the bishop and saying *Mamm* was having a breakdown. Like many things in the family, that too was forgotten, swept under the rug and never talked about again.

At least Joy was married and was out from under Levi's thumb. Good for her.

"How many buggies are we taking to the mud sale?" asked Favor.

Levi said, "I'll take one and you girls can take one. Isaac, you and Joy can come with us, or go by yourselves."

"I have to work tomorrow. I need to go there to open the place and then I'm sure I'll be able to take the rest of the day off. I'll meet you all there." Isaac looked at Joy. "Will you go there with the girls? Then you can come home with me."

"*Jah.* It'll be a lot of fun."

Bliss put her fork down and clapped her hands. "I can't wait. I don't know that I'm cut out to be Amish."

Everyone stopped what they were doing and looked at Bliss. The words had rolled off her tongue as though it was normal dinner conversation.

CHAPTER 4

CHERISH COULDN'T WORK out why Bliss would say that she didn't want to be Amish anymore, not at the dinner table and in front of her father. "Are you saying you're going on *rumspringa?*"

"I might."

"Go with Favor," Cherish suggested. "The pair of you should go together."

Favor's eyes opened wide. "I'm not going anywhere until one of my pen pals comes to stay here. *Mamm* said she'd think about it."

It was unbelievable that Favor would ever consider leaving the family home for her *rumspringa*. She was as quiet as a mouse and equally as timid. How would she make it in the big world by herself?

"*Ach*, Favor, that means no. *Mamm* will never let any of your pen pals come here," Hope said.

"I don't see why not. We have other people come to stay here. Matthew was here until recently."

"Are they *Englishers?*" asked Levi.

"Some are, but some are from communities far away."

Bliss pouted. "No one's talking about what I said about me wanting to leave."

"I can't stop you if you want to go on your *rumspringa,* Bliss," her father answered. "It's every young person's right."

"Okay then. I might do that."

"*Jah,* you might not, too," said Cherish with a giggle.

"I'll show you all. No one thinks I will do it, but I might. I know people who'll give me a place to stay."

"Can someone pass me the peas please?" asked Isaac.

Hope picked up the bowl and passed it to him.

Cherish guessed that Bliss wanted attention more than she wanted to leave the Amish or go on *rumspringa.* "Why don't you come with me next time I go to the farm, Bliss? You'll love it there, and it'll give you a break if you're wanting a change of scene."

"Okay. How long will we be there for?"

"Only a few days."

"*Denke* for inviting me. I'd love to do that. Oh, can you spare me around here, *Dat?*"

"I'm sure we can. *Mamm* will be okay with two less mouths to feed and so will my pocket."

Cherish pressed her lips together at Levi's comment. Everything with him came down to dollars. He was wealthy enough having his hand in a few investments as well as holding an interest in his brother's large farm. Why did he have to come here acting so poor, living off their apple orchard? Maybe that was how he'd become wealthy, watching every penny.

"Favor, I'll talk to *Mamm* about having one of your friends come to stay when she's better. It might not be soon, but it is a *gut* idea. The word says in Hebrews, 'Be not forgetful to entertain strangers: for thereby some have entertained angels unawares.'"

Joy added, looking smug. *"Use hospitality one to another without grudging.'* That's 1 Peter chapter four and verse nine."

Cherish couldn't stop her next words from running out of her mouth. *"Wunderbaar.* Does that mean we've just had our nightly bible study, Levi?"

"Nee, Cherish, but it has given us our subject." He turned to Isaac and Joy. "You can join us."

"Denke, but we'll have our own study."

Bliss sighed. "I hope *Mamm's* well enough for the mud sale tomorrow. I want her to get out of bed and look at what I've baked."

"When she has these migraines she's sometimes in bed for days. They knock her around pretty bad," Cherish said. "I'll go up now and see if she's been able to eat anything. Back soon." Cherish hurried away from the table before Bliss said she wanted to be the one to check on Wilma.

Cherish took the stairs two by two and then pushed open her mother's bedroom door. Her mother lay there motionless with a cold washcloth covering her forehead.

The dinner on the tray beside her was half-eaten and Cherish took that as a good sign.

"Who's there?" *Mamm* said, reaching for the washcloth.

"It's me." Cherish sat down on the side of the bed.

Wilma opened her eyes and looked at her.

"How are you feeling?"

Her mother pushed herself up in bed. "I'll be all right."

"Bliss is excited to show you her funnel cakes. They turned out pretty good."

"I'm sorry I couldn't be there to show her how to do them."

"Hope helped her. Or it could've been Joy. One of them did."

"*Gut.*"

Cherish wanted to ask her when she could go to the farm, but it wasn't the time or the place. She was so excited about Levi not objecting to her going. He'd even been okay with Favor having one of her pen pals there. Maybe Levi wasn't all bad. "We had a good dinner and everyone's getting along well."

"That's good."

"Can I get you some dessert?"

"Maybe just a cup of weak tea with sugar?"

"Sure." Cherish stood up and leaned over her mother and grabbed the tray. "Are you sure you're okay?"

"*Jah,* but I might have to stay in bed for tomorrow as well."

"I thought you would. That's too bad, you'll miss the mud sale."

"I was looking forward to going." *Mamm* picked up the washcloth and placed it back on her forehead.

When Cherish got back downstairs from looking after her mother, everyone was staring at her. "What?"

"How's *Mamm?*" Levi asked Cherish.

"Not well enough to go tomorrow. She'll need to rest. She gets very tired for days after she's had one of her migraines." She put her mother's plate on the counter beside the sink, filled up the teakettle and placed it on the stove. "Levi, can I ask Florence tomorrow about taking me to the farm?"

"*Jah,* if that's okay with your *mudder.*"

"I'll do it as soon as I get home."

Bliss stood up from the table. "Is that tea for *Mamm?*"

"*Jah.* She wants weak tea with lots of sugar."

"Can I take it up to her?"

"No. I have to ask her something."

Bliss looked upset, but that was too bad. She

27

couldn't get her own way all the time just because she was new to the family.

Cherish carried the tea carefully up the stairs. *Mamm* hated it when the tea slopped onto the saucer. When she got to the bedroom, it looked like her mother was asleep. Slowly, she lowered the cup and saucer onto the nightstand.

Then she lowered her head to listen to her mother's breathing. Her breaths were coming and going deeply; she had to be asleep, but Cherish needed an answer now. It was silly that Levi wanted *Mamm's* approval. She always jumped at the chance of getting rid of her. Levi was the one who needed convincing about things. If he approved, then her mother would too. There wasn't a doubt in her mind.

"*Mamm,*" Cherish said quietly. There was no response. "*Mamm*, Levi wants to know if I can ask Florence and Carter to take me to the farm."

She waited and then heard something. It was sort of a grunt, but she was sure it was a 'yes' grunt.

"*Denke,*" she whispered, before she went back to tell Levi that *Mamm* gave her permission.

CHAPTER 5

ONCE THEY ARRIVED at the mud sale, Cherish helped Bliss carry the funnel cakes to where Ada was selling them, and then their time was their own. Joy stayed to help Ada, and Favor joined her friends. That meant that Cherish was stuck with Bliss.

"I can't wait until the auctions start. They're so exciting. Usually *Dat* and I have things to donate but this year we had nothing. That's because we moved our whole household in with yours."

"Are you going to buy anything?"

"*Ach nee.* I don't have any money. I don't even have a job yet."

"And you won't need one if you're going on *rumspringa.*"

"Of course I will. Otherwise, how would I support myself?"

"That's true. What kind of jobs have you been looking for?"

"Anything and everything. It's not just me. Favor can't find one anywhere either. Everyone says they're not hiring. Even you can't find another job."

"I'm happy with the few shifts at the café."

Bliss gasped. "So, you're not looking for a job?"

"I have one. All I need is part-time. Levi doesn't realize it, but he needs all the help in the orchard. He can't see the forest for the trees."

"*Jah*, for all the apple trees." The two girls giggled.

Then Cherish grabbed Bliss's arm. "Look!"

Bliss looked around. "What?"

"Look at him. Do you know him?"

"Who are you looking at? You're pointing at a crowd of people."

Cherish whispered. "I'm only looking at the most handsome man I've ever seen."

Bliss narrowed her eyes. "You mean that tall one with his hat tipped back?"

"*Jah*, that's the one."

"Never seen him before. He must be from somewhere else."

"I know because no one is this handsome if they were born around here."

"*Nee*, I mean that our elders don't like the men wearing their hats back like that. It's too worldly."

Cherish wasn't listening to Bliss. "How will we

meet him? We could just walk up to him, but what will we say?"

"Just ask where he's from."

"Then what? We need more than that."

"We need someone to introduce us."

Cherish tugged on Bliss's arm. "Brilliant. We need to find someone who knows him. Let's see if Isaac's here yet. He's not from this community. He might know him. It's a good thing Mark gave him part of the day off work."

"Oh, Cherish, aren't we going to have a look at all the lovely things for sale? I can see all the beautiful quilts undercover up there."

"We will. It's not even nine yet. The quilts are among the last to be auctioned." When Bliss hesitated, Cherish added, "Don't you want me to find out my husband's name?"

Bliss giggled. "You're going to marry that stranger?"

"Why not?"

"Because I'm older than you."

"Well, he might have an older *bruder,* but that one's mine. I saw him first. I don't care that I'll have to wait a few years." Cherish charged ahead holding onto Bliss's arm so she had no option but to follow.

"ISAAC!"

He swung around. "Cherish, and Bliss. Hi. Are you looking for Joy?"

Bliss pushed in front. "Cherish has seen her future husband and she's hoping you know him. He's not from around here."

Isaac looked over at Cherish and she felt her cheeks burning. It wasn't often that she got embarrassed, but Bliss had done a thorough job of it. "Can we point him out to you, and you tell us if you know him?" asked Cherish.

He laughed. "Sure. Where is he?"

Cherish looked around and couldn't see him. "I'll have to find him."

"I'll follow," said Isaac.

They weaved their way in and out of the crowd until they saw him talking with someone. "There. That's him." Cherish nodded toward him.

"Can't say that I know him. *Nee,* I'm sure I don't."

Cherish's fingers nervously fiddled with her *kapp* strings. How was she going to talk to the man? This would be awkward. Then she saw him move behind the counter. He was selling something. "Okay, you two can go now." Without looking behind her, Cherish moved forward. Then she saw he was standing behind rabbits in a cage.

Their eyes locked.

She stood still for a moment, and then she slowly walked toward him.

"Hello," he said.

She said a quiet hello back and then she caught sight of the rabbits in a cage by his feet. "What are you doing with those?"

"I'm selling the baby rabbits. For pets, of course, and nothing else."

"Rabbits for pets?" To her, rabbits were vermin, pests in the orchard, and to all the farms 'round about.

"I have babies. Come take a look." He moved behind one of the larger cages and crouched down and then she joined him.

There was another cage with six baby rabbits. "They're so cute."

"I'm fond of rabbits. They make the best pets."

"Interesting."

"Are you looking for a pet?"

She looked up at him. His eyes glinted in the morning sun and it also highlighted the hair sticking out from under his hat. It was honey brown with streaks of gold. Up close, he was the most beautiful man she'd ever seen. Was this man her future husband?

CHAPTER 6

CHERISH REALIZED THE HANDSOME MAN,
possibly her future husband, had asked her a question.
"I might be looking for a pet."

Mamm will kill me if I bring another pet home! screamed
the voice inside her head.

She'd not yet heard the end of it from back when
she brought their late Aunt Dagmar's bird home. Now,
though, she had to keep the conversation going.
"You're not from around here, are you?" she offered
him a charming smile, knowing it worked on
most men.

"Not yet. I'm moving here. I got myself a job
working with a friend of a friend. That's only for a few
weeks and then I've got a job doing construction with a
friend of my uncle."

"That's a lot of friends. You must be a friendly
person."

He chuckled. "I guess so."

"I've lived here all my life. You'll love it here."

He grinned at her, revealing straight white teeth. "I'm starting to see that. I'm coming back at the end of the week after next."

Perfect! A handsome Amish man, and by the sounds of it, a hard-working one.

She crouched down and looked at the gray and brown rabbits once more. If he was coming back soon, she'd need to get to the farm and back by then or he'd be snatched up by another single girl. The wheels in her mind started turning as she planned. She needed to be right there when he moved, and she could even offer to show him around. "You say they make good pets?"

He crouched down next to her. "Sure do. They use a litter tray and everything. Also, they're cleaner than cats. They're forever grooming themselves."

"One would be perfect for Bliss."

"Excuse me, did you say 'for bliss?'"

"Oh, Bliss is my half-sister. No wait, she's my step-sister. My mother recently remarried, and I have a new stepfather and a new stepsister. I do have a half-sister, too. Her name's Florence and she lives next door now. She married an *Englisher.*" Cherish stopped abruptly when she heard herself babbling nervously like Favor usually did.

He smiled at her, his lips twisted, hinting at amusement.

She took the smile as a good thing and kept going.

"Anyway, Bliss said she wants a pet, but it's not her birthday for some time. Where would I hide it until then?"

"When's her birthday?"

Cherish lowered her head while she thought. With all Bliss's carrying on about her birthday, Cherish had failed to take in when the actual date was. "It's in a couple of weeks and I could give it to her early, but that kind of ruins things, don't you think?"

"Most definitely. If it's a birthday present it should be given on the exact day. Not a day before and not a day after."

"My thoughts exactly." They locked eyes with one another. Cherish hoped he was feeling something too. She studied his face to see if he was just playing along with her in an effort to offload a rabbit. It was hard to tell. Just when she was thinking what to do with the rabbit and what *Mamm* would say to the introduction of one into the household, he spoke.

"How about you choose one and I'll look after it for you and bring it back with me?" He stood and then she stood up too.

Perfect! That way there was a reason to meet up with him as soon as he got back. "Okay. *Wunderbaar, denke.*" She stared down at the rabbits. "I don't know which one to choose." There was an annoying one jumping all over the others and it reminded her of Bliss. "That one would suit her best."

He chuckled. "I call him, Bruiser. He's a real trouble

maker and I think he's got the prettiest markings. All white with just the one patch on one side."

"Yes, he is pretty. Bruiser would be perfect. Even better that he's a boy. He is for certain, isn't he? I'd prefer a boy over a girl."

"I'd say so. As far as I can tell."

"How much?" She looked in the small fabric bag she had slung over her shoulder. She had fifty dollars she'd secretly kept aside from her wages. Although they had to give all their pay to Levi, he didn't know about her tips. She was keeping that part to herself.

He grinned at her. "A dollar."

She looked up at him in shock. *"Nee.* How much is the rabbit, and then for you feeding him while you look after him?"

"A dollar." His lips twisted into a smile.

"That's not the true price."

"It is. That's the price for you."

"I can't let you do that. You're selling these to make money."

"Okay."

She held her breath hoping he wasn't going to say a figure higher than fifty.

"Alright then. A dollar, plus your word that you'll go on a buggy ride with me as soon as I get back and settled here."

Cherish couldn't stop the giggle that escaped her lips. He had to think she was older than she was, but that didn't bother her in the least. She'd tell him once he was hooked on her—in love with her. She knew she looked just as old as her sisters, and many people thought she was eighteen or more. Putting out her hand, she said, "I feel bad about you giving him to me for such a low amount, but it's a deal."

He wrapped his warm fingers around her small hand. She looked down at their clasped hands as tingles of electricity shot through her.

"What's your last name?" He released her hand far too soon for her liking.

"Baker. I'm Cherish Baker."

"Where do you live?"

"Bakers' Apple Orchard. Just ask anyone. Everyone in town knows where that is. We're quite well known."

"I love apples."

Cherish giggled again. "Me too. What's your name?"

"Adam Wengerd."

People coming forward to look at the rabbits interrupted them right when Cherish was rehearsing her future name in her mind. *Cherish Wengerd.* She could get used to that.

"I'll find you when I come back here, Cherish Baker from Bakers' Apple Orchard."

"Okay." They exchanged smiles and she walked away not watching where she was going and was nearly knocked over by someone leading two horses. The scare brought her back to reality with a thud. Bliss came charging toward her and looped an arm through hers.

"Tell me everything."

"His name's Adam Wengerd. He wants to see me. He's moving here." Her fingertips flew to her mouth. "That means it's even more important that I get to the farm and back before he gets here. Oh, I hope Florence agrees to take me. She does like it at the farm and so does Carter, and they usually agree to take me. They have whenever I've asked, but now she's pregnant. I hope that doesn't make a difference."

"What did Adam say exactly? Tell me everything from the first word to the last."

"I can tell you this. He wants me to go on a buggy ride with him."

Bliss gasped. *"Ach,* you're too young. *Dat* would never allow it."

Cherish stopped walking and glared at her stepsister, who had to stop too since their arms were still linked. "He won't know, and you won't tell him."

"I can't lie to my own *vadder."*

Cherish kept walking. "You won't have to. Just don't say anything. He'll never think of asking."

"I don't know."

Cherish pulled her arm out of Bliss's grasp. "We can't be friends if you double-cross me." She fixed her fists onto her hips. "You asked me, so I told you, but only because I trusted you."

"Okay. I won't say anything." Bliss nodded. "You can trust me."

Cherish smiled and Bliss took hold of her arm again.

"You found someone nice now let's look for someone for me. Someone tall and someone who makes me laugh. He has to be kind too, and caring. He doesn't have to be the most handsome man, but he has to think I'm the most beautiful woman he's ever laid eyes on." Bliss giggled.

"Now where will we find a man like that?" Cherish had no interest in helping Bliss, but she forced herself to be nice since Bliss was keeping her secret about Adam.

"There are hundreds of men here. My husband could easily be here today. Let's see who's watching the auction." They walked over to the crowd of people that had gathered.

"They all look the same if you ask me." Cherish was losing interest fast. Then she spotted Isaac. "What about that man over there talking with Isaac?"

"He looks a little old."

"He's not married though, since he's clean-shaven. Come on." She hurried toward Isaac who was standing talking to the stranger.

CHAPTER 7

ISAAC STOPPED TALKING when they approached, and the other man looked on.

"Excuse me, Isaac, but have you seen Joy?"

"*Jah,* she's helping Ada with the cake stall." Isaac glanced at his friend, and then looked back at the girls. "Have you all met?"

"*Nee,* we haven't," the stranger said smiling at the girls.

His light brown hair was tinged with strawberry-blond highlights and his skin was paler than most men's. His eyes were the bluest of blue.

"I'm Cherish and this is Bliss."

"Pleased to meet you both. I'm Daniel. I'm from the same community as Isaac."

"That's nice and you're here for the mud sale?" asked Cherish.

"No. I'm traveling around visiting."

"And how long will you be here for, Daniel?" Bliss asked.

"A couple of weeks I'd say. Depending on how long I feel like. I've got no set routine. That's the way I like it."

Cherish turned up her nose. "Oh, then you don't know where you're going in life?"

"Cherish," Bliss admonished her with a nudge.

He laughed. "That's okay. After I travel, I'll settle down and start my own business."

"Around here?" Bliss asked.

"I'll go home."

"That sounds like a good idea, traveling around. I might like to do that too." She turned to Cherish. "Do you think Favor would like to come with me?"

Cherish frowned at her. "You think Levi would allow you to go anywhere?"

"You have a husband, Bliss?" The disappointment on Daniel's face revealed some interest in Bliss.

Bliss giggled and her cheeks flushed scarlet. "I'm not even old enough to be married. Nearly old enough, but not quite. Levi is my father."

"That's what I thought at first." Daniel smiled at her.

"Who are you staying with?"

"Ada and Samuel."

"Ah, we know them very well. Ada and my mother are the best of friends. She often has people stay with her."

Cherish stared at Bliss wanting her to say something. Maybe invite him for dinner.

"We might see you around, then. At the meeting on Sunday," said Bliss.

"I hope so," Daniel said, smiling.

The two girls moved away.

When they were a good distance, Cherish asked, "Well, what did you think?"

"I didn't feel anything."

"Nothing?"

"*Nee.*"

"Oh, that's too bad."

"Should I have felt something?"

"I guess so. Did you think he was handsome?"

Bliss shook her head. "Not really if I'm honest."

"Well, you should be honest. But you said you didn't need someone to be handsome."

"I know. Let's just forget him, shall we?"

Now she was feeling even more impatient with Bliss. Daniel was perfect and he'd be easy to get to know since he was staying with Ada. "Okay. If that's what you want. Although, it would be convenient with him staying where he is."

"*Jah,* but he's opening a business in another town. I want to stay here with *Dat,* and all of you and the girls too, of course. Let's forget about finding someone for me and we'll just enjoy our day."

"Suits me just fine."

After they walked around for a while, Bliss stopped still.

"What is it?" Cherish asked.

"Look who's talking to Isaac now. Isn't that the man you were talking with before, the one with his hat tipped back?"

"*Jah,* it is."

"Let's see what they're talking about." Before Cherish could stop her, Bliss walked up to Isaac.

Isaac smiled at them when they walked up, stopping his conversation mid-sentence. "Adam, have you met Cherish and Bliss?"

Adam smiled at Cherish. "I've met Cherish, but I haven't met Bliss." He gave Cherish a quick nod to let her know he'd remembered Bliss was the one who would be receiving the surprise birthday bunny.

"Bliss, this is Adam."

"Nice to meet you, Adam."

He nodded. "You too."

"You know each other?" Bliss asked.

"Adam's coming back the week after next to help me in the saddlery store for a while, and he'll be staying at Mark and Christina's."

Cherish frowned and looked at Isaac. He'd just said he didn't know Adam. What was going on? More importantly, why was he helping in the store? "Why's that? What about Mark?"

"Mark and Christina are going away. Adam is coming back in two weeks to help out."

Cherish placed her hands on her hips. Mark would've known her sisters were looking for work and Isaac definitely knew. "Is that right?"

"He never mentioned anything to us, and we had them over for dinner just last week," Bliss said.

Isaac shrugged his shoulders. "They just made up their minds in the last few days. It sounds like Christina's thinking about a change."

"She's thinking of moving and taking Mark away?" Cherish wanted to burst into tears. After her father died, her older half brother, Earl, moved away and if they were to lose Mark to a different community it would feel like losing both Earl and *Dat* all over again.

"Mark doesn't want to move because he's got the store. He's just trying to keep Christina happy."

"That's not an easy thing to do." The words had slipped right out of Cherish's mouth and she got a sharp dig in the ribs from Bliss. The second one in the last couple of hours.

"I didn't mean that like it sounded, obviously," Cherish said trying to cover up.

Isaac jumped in, rescuing her. "Adam and I just got to talking and then I realized who Adam was. All I knew was his name. Now I can put a face to the name."

That explained it.

Adam kept smiling at her.

"When you said you were working here, Adam, I didn't know you were working in my brother's store," Cherish said.

"Me neither. I mean, I did know where I'd be working, but I didn't know Mark was your brother."

"I'll look forward to seeing more of you." Adam smiled at her, while she could see Isaac frowning at her comment. What was wrong with being friendly?

Behind them the auction got loud. When the uproar of the crowd died down, Bliss said, "Let's have a look to see what the fuss is about."

Cherish hurried over with her and the men stayed put. They watched as the auctioneer auctioned off everything from a kitchen stool to an Amish quilt to horses. All the proceeds were going to the local volunteer firefighters.

Once there was a break in the auction, Cherish got bored. "Let's talk to Ada and ask her to dinner for Monday. *Mamm* will be better by then and you can get to know Daniel better."

"I don't know about that, Cherish. I don't think I like him."

"You can't tell by looking. You've got to get to know him better. It's just being polite having people over for dinner."

"I suppose you're right."

Cherish had another reason she wanted Daniel to like Bliss, and Bliss to like Daniel. She'd invited Bliss to the farm, but she would've preferred her stepsister didn't go. She wanted to go alone, just herself with Carter and Florence like she'd done before. There was also the problem of what would happen if Bliss was attracted to Malachi and he became attracted to her. What if they fell in love with one another? Then she'd never be rid of Malachi from her life. That wouldn't do at all. Malachi had to be kept away from her sisters and her stepsister.

"*Jah*, you're right I will get to know him." Bliss turned around to stare at him. "He doesn't seem too bad."

"He's not. He's lovely, really nice. I don't know why you're being so offhand about him. You should be more excited. I'm sure he'll like you too when he gets to know you."

Bliss covered her mouth and giggled. "I hope so."

"Seems like it to me."

"Come on. Let's go invite Ada for dinner Monday night." Cherish charged off to the food table where Ada was raising money selling pies and funnel cakes.

When they got there, they waited until Ada finished serving a lady and then jumped right in. "Ada, we'd love for you to come to dinner Monday night."

Ada narrowed her eyes. "Cherish, this is the first time you've invited me to dinner. It's normally your *mudder*."

"Mmm, I don't think I have. Oh well, there's always a first time for everything."

"Would this have anything to do with the young man we have staying with us?"

"You have a guest?" Cherish answered as innocently as she could.

49

Bliss burst out laughing and hid behind Cherish, and then Cherish couldn't keep the smile from her face. "Whoever your visitor is, why not bring them along?"

"Would your *mudder* be alright with that, then? I heard she's not too well."

"She'd be over it by then. She's just got a migraine."

"It's not *just* a migraine, Cherish, she gets *dreadful* migraines." Bliss stepped out from behind her.

"I know, Bliss. Saying that made me sound uncaring and I'm not. I didn't mean it like that. What I meant was, they don't usually last more than a day or two. Three at the most."

"As long as you're sure she'll be over it by then and she won't be doing any of the cooking, will she? You girls will help?" Ada arched an eyebrow, looking at both girls.

"I'll check with *Mamm* and then let you know tomorrow at the meeting."

"Fine. *Denke* for the kind invitation, Cherish. I take it you've met Daniel?"

Bliss was laughing again, so Cherish had to be the one to admit it. "*Jah,* we have met Daniel and we think he's very nice. And we just wanted to be friendly didn't we, Bliss?"

"*Jah,* we just wanted to be friendly."

"Very good. Now next time that's exactly what you can say. You don't need to be all deceptive like that, Cherish."

"I'm sorry, Ada, I wasn't meaning to be deceptive. I

mean, I can see how you'd think that. We did know Daniel was staying with you. We should've said that outright."

"At least you admitted it. You are getting better with your honesty. You've given your *mamm* a lot of trouble over the years."

Ada always had a way of making Cherish feel bad about herself. And here she was trying to do a nice thing for Bliss. "I'll see you tomorrow then, Ada, after I talked to *Mamm*."

"Very good. I'll talk to you tomorrow, girls." Ada turned from them and started to serve customers.

CHAPTER 8

FLORENCE SETTLED herself in the living room with the sun streaming through the narrow window. After she popped her feet up on the coffee table, she picked up the baby jacket she was knitting. She was more of a seamstress than a knitter. And even though she was blessed with them having enough money to buy any baby clothes they wanted, knitting some of them was a pleasant way to pass the time. She had various knitting projects in mind. Firstly, would be the jacket and then there were a couple of dressy outfits that she liked and that would suit either a boy or a girl.

Every time she sat down to knit or sew, she missed Wilma and her half-sisters and the nights they'd sit and work on their crafts together. There would be a lot of talking, a lot of laughing and, more often than not there'd be arguments. Then Wilma and Florence would be the last ones up sewing into the night.

Even though Florence was blissfully happy in her marriage to Carter it didn't stop her missing her old family at times. Wilma and Levi had no interest in keeping in contact, but she was grateful that they didn't stop the girls from talking to her.

She looked down at the knitting. With each stitch, she was closer to giving birth, closer to holding their baby in her arms, and closer to feeling like she had a complete family.

WHEN THE DAY of the mud sale was over and the girls were back at home, Cherish sprinted through the orchard to visit her older half-sister, Florence. She slipped through the barbed wire fence and hurried to the cottage. The car was there so that meant that both Carter and Florence were at home. It was just after four in the afternoon. The other girls stayed at home, too worried about their mother to join her.

"Bonnet Sister approaching," Carter called out from his upstairs office.

"Which one is it?" Florence asked.

"Trouble."

"Ah, Cherish." Florence smiled as she opened the front door. Cherish was just walking up the porch steps.

"Hello, Florence. I can never get used to seeing you in those clothes and with your hair uncovered."

"Hello. Me too. I am still sometimes surprised when I see my reflection in town and realize it's me." The two women embraced. "Come inside."

"Is Carter home?"

"Sure am." He moved quickly down the stairs and then met Cherish with a hug. "Now let me guess why you're here. There's been some disaster at home?" He tapped his chin. "No, that's not it because you're not crying. So … I'd say you want us to drive you to your farm?"

Cherish giggled. "I didn't know I was that obvious."

"Just a little bit. I'll leave you with Florence. I've got work to catch up on."

She grabbed him by the arm as he was walking away. "But what about …"

He turned and smiled as he took hold of her hand and put it back down by her side. "Florence can make that decision. I'll fit into whatever the both of you decide."

"Thanks, Carter."

He gave her a nod before he went back up the stairs.

"Sit down," said Florence leading Cherish to the living room. Once they were both seated, Florence asked the obvious question. "Is that why you're here, about going to the farm?"

Cherish was disappointed in herself. It seemed that the only reason she came to visit them was when she wanted something. In any other circumstances, she would've said she was just seeing how they were and then she'd come back in a few days, but she was under time constraints. "The thing is, I need to go there soon if that's okay."

"How soon?"

"Next week, even this week, maybe?"

"How about this week, this coming Wednesday? I have a medical appointment Tuesday and if all is well, we can leave on Wednesday morning."

"Perfect! And how is the little *boppli* doing?" Cherish reached over and patted Florence's tummy. "Will you find out if it's a boy or a girl?"

"Yes. If we want to know we can find out. We don't know if we want to know yet."

"A surprise is nice, but if you know, it's easier to make plans and I'm sure we'll all want to sew and knit you things. Joy has already started. Although I'm not so sure that she's not sewing clothes for her own *boppli* for when it arrives. Not that she's pregnant yet, but I'm sure she's hoping. *Ach nee,* I'm rambling like Favor. That's the second time I've done that today." She leaned back into the couch and looked up at the ceiling. "What if I'm turning into my *schweschder?*"

Florence giggled. "You seem the same to me."

Cherish sat upright. "*Denke,* so much and thank Carter for me too. I'm so excited about going back to the farm."

"Might that have anything to do with a certain young man?"

Cherish stared at Florence. How could she possibly know about the man with the rabbits? "What man?"

"Malachi."

"*Pfft.*" Cherish scoffed. "Malachi is my worst nightmare. I only hope he hasn't ruined the farm."

"He's doing a wonderful job and you should tell him so. Don't take your anger out on him."

"I have no anger. Well, maybe a little bit. I suppose I do." They'd all had a better life when their father was still alive. Things had gone downhill for everyone since then.

Florence continued, "I think you're frustrated about the farm, that you can't be there yourself until you're older ... and you're resenting Malachi because he's there running the farm when you want to do it."

"Yeah, I guess that's true. That's pretty clever of you to work that out, Florence."

"It wasn't too hard. Don't try to flatter me. I already said we'd take you."

Cherish smiled, grateful to her older sister. They hadn't always gotten along, but Florence was the one person she knew she could rely upon. That was something that hadn't changed. "I'll be nice to Malachi, and I'll even compliment him for all the things he's done right."

"That'd be a good start."

"So, I'll come back soon to check how your appointment went and if all is good, we leave on Wednesday morning?"

"Yes."

Cherish leaned forward and wrapped her arms around Florence. *"Denke,* so much."

"You're welcome. I do hope you've asked *Mamm* and Levi, though. I don't want there to be any problems or misunderstandings. Carter and I are trying to avoid dramas as best we can." She patted her tummy.

"Mamm has one of her migraines and Levi said it was okay."

"Good. Not good about *Mamm* having a migraine, though. That's not good."

"I know. She had it yesterday and you know how she's always so tired for a few days after that."

Florence nodded. "I saw Levi working in the orchard the other day."

Cherish's face lit up. She'd forgotten to tell her about Levi's change of heart as far as the orchard was concerned. "He got a book out of the library and then bought himself a copy, and he's now agreed to keeping the orchard organic."

Florence's face broke into a bright smile. "My prayers have been answered. Spraying so close to our orchard would've affected our trees." She looked up to the ceiling and said a silent prayer of thanks. "This is a true miracle. Is he listening to you girls? You all probably know more than you realize."

Cherish nodded. "I think he might be more open to listening to us now he's got that book. We did tell him it was overdue to harvest the apples last year."

"Ah, don't remind me of what a disaster that was."

"Yeah. We lost a lot of money and now Levi is focused on saving every penny, even more so than he was before. When will you be planting your trees? I don't see anything happening."

Florence sighed. "Everything seems to be going so slow, but it's important to get the preparation right. The drainage is done and now we're onto the soil preparation. It'll take several years until we have a good orchard like the one you have."

"The one Levi has, you mean."

"I didn't want to say that out loud."

"Me either, but I must say he is improving, which is not saying much." Cherish giggled.

"Do you still have to give him all your wages?"

"*Jah*, but I keep my tips. He doesn't know about them. I get a lot too, because I'm very nice to my customers. They love me."

"Ah, best you keep quiet about the tips, then."

"I will." Cherish giggled again. "I better get home and see about cooking dinner or I'll get accused that I'm lazy." She bounded to her feet and leaned over and hugged Florence. "Don't get up. I'll show myself out." When Cherish straightened up, she yelled out, "Bye, Carter."

"Bye, Cherish," Carter called down from upstairs.

When Cherish got back home, she found Bliss, Favor and Hope busy in the kitchen, with *Mamm* sitting in the living room in front of the fire. Seeing her sisters had everything under control, she went to talk to her mother. "You look cozy, *Mamm,* all covered in a blanket by the fire and in your lovely brown dressing gown."

"Here you are, you silly girl."

Cherish's breath caught in her throat as she stared at her mother. What had she done now?

She hurried to sit next to her mother. "What have I done, or not done?"

"No one knew where you had gone."

"Oh, is that all?"

"*Jah.*"

"Well, I did tell someone, I'm sure of it. I told them I was asking Carter and Florence if they'd take me back to the farm for a couple of days. It's important I keep checking or who knows what Malachi will do. I told you he sold off all the chickens, didn't I?"

"*Jah* you told me all about the horrible things Malachi did. You talk about him a lot." Wilma put her head back onto the couch and closed her eyes.

Cherish could see her mother was still in some pain and that was probably why she was being mean and calling her silly. "I have to. I've got a responsibility weighing heavily on my shoulders, *Mamm.* I've got the whole farm to run and be responsible for."

"If it's too much for you, share the farm with your sisters. That's what should've happened in the first place. It never should've been that Dagmar played favorites."

"I know you're not happy she left the farm to me,

but that's what she wanted. I'm not going to share it with anyone. It's all mine. Aunt Dagmar and I really got along. We were like twins, separated by the generations."

Mamm's lips pressed together. "You weren't like twins. You were nothing alike. We sent you there to straighten your behavior. Dagmar wouldn't have messed up one day in her life. She would never have been caught sneaking off with boys at three in the morning."

"I didn't mean that. We were like twins in other ways."

"I can't see it. You were opposites."

Cherish felt a warm glow when she thought about the good times she'd had with Dagmar and all the farm skills Dagmar taught her. "I hated her at first, and hated you and Florence for sending me there, but it was the best thing ever. I can't imagine never getting to know Dagmar. I'm so grateful you sent me there. I know it was meant to be a punishment, but it wasn't. Not really. She was really special."

"Humph. She was fierce and cranky. That was why we sent you there. We knew she wouldn't stand for your nonsense."

Cherish giggled as she remembered back to her first days at Dagmar's. "The farm was so much work, there was no time for trouble and nowhere to go to get into trouble."

"That was the idea. You were away from men."

Cherish placed her head on her mother's shoulder. "I want to be just like Dagmar when I grow up."

"An old maid?"

"*Nee,* not that part. She was never lonely because she had all the animals. They were her friends."

"I'm sure she would've rather had a family if she'd had a choice. Maybe she lived so isolated that she never met anyone."

"Maybe."

"You should never move there unless you want to be a spinster too."

"I will live there as soon as I can leave here."

Her mother moved to stare at her. "Why is it you never listen to me? I can't remember one time in your life where you've taken my advice."

"I don't know. I can't answer that. Maybe we're just too different."

"Get me a cup of tea would you, Cherish?"

"Sure."

Cherish jumped to her feet and headed out to the kitchen. Her mother was right. She always questioned everything, not content to follow along with the crowd, she wasn't sure why. In the kitchen she saw Hope stirring something on the stove and noticed Bliss in the large dining room, that adjoined the kitchen, setting the table. "Need any help in here?" she asked no one in particular.

Hope spun around. "*Nee,* we're fine."

"Can you put the teakettle on for *Mamm?* She needs a cup of hot tea."

"I'll do it," said Bliss, leaving the cutlery on the table. "And I'll take it out to her."

"Good then I'll—"

"You can start washing up those dishes there. If we don't clear them away, we'll have a mountain to get through after dinner."

Cherish pouted. She had hoped to sneak away and get out of work. With so many sisters and her being the youngest, it was generally easy to leave things for someone else. "Sure." Cherish fixed a smile on her face and walked toward the dishes, pushing up her sleeves.

CHAPTER 9

HOPE GOT on her bike on Monday after work and pedaled home. She could not get her mind off Fairfax. All the what-ifs and what could've beens ran through her mind. Should she have expressed her disappointment in him not talking to the bishop when he said he would? It was only reasonable that he talk things over with his parents. That was only being respectful. Perhaps now he thought of her as unreasonable and demanding when she wasn't. Was she?

Had she ruined things forever?

Frustration gnawed at her heart while her stomach churned. It didn't help that she hadn't eaten anything all day, and had eaten very little the day before. How could she enjoy food when she was unsure of her future?

She missed him so much. All she wanted was to see him. Just a glimpse would make her feel better. Hope had a plan. If she went through the back of her family's orchard, she might see him outside his cottage or working in his orchard.

When she got as close as she could to his cottage, shielded by the trees, she scanned everywhere for him. His pickup truck was parked outside his cottage, but he was nowhere to be seen. On a day like today, he should've been working in the orchard somewhere. From where she stood, only a section of the neighboring orchard could be seen. She leaned her bike against a tree and climbed up one of the apple trees until she was a few feet higher.

Still, she saw nothing.

Hope jumped to the ground and dusted her hands off, grabbed the handlebars of her bike and started off toward home. It was hard not seeing him these past few days when she'd seen him twice a day for the last few months, except for Sundays. For the first time, she considered leaving her family and the community for him and then she discounted it just as fast. She couldn't be on the outside.

She wheeled her bike toward home still staying close to the Jenkins' border fence shielded by the trees so she wouldn't be seen by anyone from the neighboring property. Before she got too far away, she stopped, closed her eyes and prayed that if it was *Gott's* will they would end up together.

A sense of peace washed over her taking away her pain and hurt. She had to believe that God held her future in His hands; He would not let her down. If Fairfax was not the one for her then surely God would have someone better, and that man would be someone wonderful if he was better than Fairfax.

When she opened her eyes, she looked back at his cottage, which by now was small in the distance.

When she got back to her house, she joined Bliss and Cherish who were peeling vegetables at the kitchen table.

In an effort to take her mind off Fairfax, she sat down with them. They'd stopped talking as soon as she walked into the kitchen. "What are you two talking about?"

Cherish said, "I was just saying to Bliss she might want to give some more thought about coming to the farm."

"Why's that?" asked Hope.

"There's this man, Daniel. He's coming to dinner tonight. You'll meet him. He's staying with Ada and Samuel. Didn't you meet him yesterday at the meeting?"

"Nee, I didn't. There were a few visitors. I didn't pay much attention. I should've. So, you like him, Bliss?"

"I might. I'm not sure. I'll wait and see what happens tonight."

"If she likes him, she shouldn't waste time going to the farm with me. I'll be upset, but it'll be for the best for Bliss." Cherish smiled sweetly, but something told

Hope that it would really be better for Cherish if Bliss stayed home.

"Oh, I want to see the farm. You're always talking about the farm and I've never been there."

Cherish swallowed hard. "I thought you'd want to stay here and get to know him because he won't be here for much longer. I go there every few months. I'll take you next time."

Bliss nodded. "Okay."

Then Cherish leaned forward and whispered. "Who knows? By that time you might be engaged to Daniel."

"*Jah*, I suppose it's possible."

Now Hope got to thinking about Fairfax again. She grabbed a slice of raw carrot and popped it into her mouth.

"It certainly would be. And you could encourage him to stay in this community and open that business he's thinking about."

"I could, couldn't I?"

"*Jah*, for certain," Cherish said. "Now, you'll have to let him know in a subtle way that you've cooked this dinner all by yourself. *Mamm's* not well enough, so Levi won't mind that she didn't cook the meal."

"*Jah*, he likes it when she cooks it," Bliss said. "But you're helping me."

"Not that much," Cherish said. "I'm hardly doing a thing. It's not even enough to mention. You must impress Daniel with your cooking. Men like to know their future *fraa* can cook well."

"Oh. Do you think so?"

"*Jah.* He won't want to starve. Isn't that right, Hope?"

"If you say so."

Cherish stared at Hope. "What's wrong with you?"

"Nothing."

Bliss chimed in, "You haven't been yourself, Hope."

"I'm all right." Hope stood. "I'll be in my room since you and Bliss are cooking the dinner tonight, Cherish." She hurried away so they wouldn't be able to ask her more questions.

CHAPTER 10

As soon as everything was cooking, Cherish asked Bliss, "Have you thought about what you're going to wear?"

Bliss looked at her clothes. "I had planned on just wearing this."

Cherish grimaced looking her up and down. "I don't think so. It won't do at all. You've got to dress up and look the best that you possibly can. You have a nicer dress than that, so wear it."

"I was keeping that one clean to wear for the next meeting."

"That's not for ages. It's only Monday. Come up with me and I'll have a look at what you've got. You might even be able to squeeze your porky self into one of mine."

Bliss opened her mouth in shock. Cherish grabbed

her hand and they headed upstairs to the bedroom, leaving the food to cook.

Bliss ended up insisting on wearing her Sunday best even though she'd worn it the day before.

When Cherish saw their guests arrive, she advised Bliss to stay in the kitchen while she opened the door. *Mamm* was better and had joined them for dinner, and Joy and Isaac joined them as well. Even though Christina and Mark had been invited, they gave an excuse why they couldn't come. Cherish knew it was because they didn't want to talk about exactly why they were going away. Their trip away was shrouded in mystery. Eventually, Cherish would find out why, but right now she was more interested in matching Bliss with Daniel.

Cherish had told the guests where to sit, and had arranged it so Daniel and Bliss would be sitting together. "Daniel, you can sit here next to Levi since you're our special guest. And Bliss you can sit next to Daniel. Is that okay, Daniel?"

"Sure."

Cherish noticed Daniel looked more than a little pleased about this.

Her plan was working well until Levi asked, "Why are you cooking tonight, Bliss?"

Bliss stared at her father from within the kitchen and no words came out.

Cherish had to help her. "Bliss doesn't have a chance to show off her cooking very often. She's such a good cook. *Mamm* needs a break too considering her recent migraine." She looked at Levi hoping he'd agree, but he said nothing, just gave a grunt. Cherish slumped into her chair almost at the point of giving up. If Bliss didn't like Daniel better at the end of the night, she'd give up. This was hard work! She could lead a horse to water but she couldn't make her drink.

Once all the food was on the table and everyone was seated, they all closed their eyes for the silent prayer. Slowly, Cherish opened one eye to look at Daniel and Bliss. They did look like they would make a good pair.

When the prayers were done, the bowls of food were passed around. Everyone served their own portions of food. That's normally how they ate when they had people over.

"It'll be my birthday soon," Bliss blurted out.

"That's *wunderbaar,*" Daniel said to her, even though he'd probably heard that already. That's all Bliss could talk about.

It was up to Cherish to change the subject fast. She'd scream if Bliss mentioned her birthday one more time. "What did everybody think about the mud sale on Saturday?"

"*Wunderbaar,*" said Samuel, Ada's husband. "They raised a record amount of money."

Wilma said, "Each year they make more than the last."

"It's a shame you weren't well enough to go, *Mamm,*" said Bliss smiling at Wilma.

73

"I know. Perhaps I'll make it to the next one, *Gott* willing."

"And what do you do for work, Daniel?" asked Levi, staring at him, sizing him up, as only a potential *vadder*-in-law would.

"Whatever I can, really. A bit of this and a bit of that. Construction mainly."

Levi gave a nod of approval. "Every man should know how to build."

"It's true," added Samuel.

"What about you, Mr. Bruner?" asked Daniel.

"I work this apple orchard. Before that, my brother and I had three farms between us. We sold them and now we only have one, which my brother runs. We also have a few other interests, but I won't talk about that. The women at the table wouldn't want to know about it."

The conversation was as boring as it could be, but the real opportunity would come at the end of the meal. Cherish hoped that Daniel and Bliss would have a private time to talk and get to know one another.

When dessert was over, the opportunity came. Joy and Isaac excused themselves and went home, and then the younger half of the guests stayed on the porch enjoying a conversation by the soft lighting of two gas lamps. The older folk went inside to sit more comfortably in the living room.

Cherish made sure that Bliss stayed close to Daniel, and when they started talking, she moved to the other end of the porch with Hope and Favor. One ear was still on Bliss and Daniel. She couldn't hear everything that was said, but by the occasional giggle and Bliss's smiling face, she knew they were getting along fine.

It seemed hopeful now that Cherish would go to the farm alone with just Carter and Florence. She liked to be alone in the car with them during the long drive to the farm and back. Her plan worked much better than telling Bliss outright she changed her mind and didn't want her to tag along.

When Cherish went inside to ask everyone if they wanted another cup of tea, Ada and Samuel announced they were going home. Since they had brought Daniel in the buggy with them that meant he had to go with them.

"Are you sure you don't want to stay a little longer?" asked Cherish.

"*Nee*, it's getting late and your *mudder* could probably do with an early night."

Mamm just sat there not speaking up. Eventually, Wilma said, "I'll walk out with you."

Cherish and her family waited on the porch and waved goodbye to Ada, Samuel and their guest.

Once they were out of sight, Cherish said to Bliss. "Let's get the dishes out of the way, shall we?"

"*Jah*. It won't take long."

"Everyone else can go to bed," Cherish said.

"*Denke*, girls," Wilma said.

75

"You did good tonight, Bliss. The food was wonderful wasn't it, Wilma?" Levi asked.

"It was. You made a nice meal, Bliss."

Bliss hurried over and hugged Wilma.

Wilma responded by putting an arm loosely around Bliss's shoulder. "I should go to bed."

"Night, *Mamm,*" Bliss said when Wilma moved away.

"Gut nacht, girls."

Levi and Wilma headed up the stairs.

Now Cherish could get to work convincing Bliss how fine a man Daniel was. It was true, he was, and just as well. "You two can go to bed. Bliss and I will clean up," Cherish told Hope and Favor.

"You sure?" Hope asked.

Favor pulled on Hope's sleeve. "Don't ask them. Let's just go."

Hope smiled. "Okay. An early night sounds *gut* to me."

After Hope and Favor were gone, Bliss and Cherish brought the used coffee cups into the kitchen, and then began a final clearing of the large dinner table.

Cherish was waiting for Bliss to talk about Daniel; she'd not said a thing. "What do you think of him?"

"Daniel?"

"Yeah, who else?"

A big smile puffed out Bliss's cheeks. "I think he's *wunderbaar.*"

"Didn't I tell you?"

76

"Yah. He is very nice. But he didn't arrange a time to see me again. Wouldn't he have done that if he really liked me? We were alone there on the porch. That was a perfect time to ask me on a buggy ride or to meet him somewhere."

"Not necessarily. Not if he didn't know what he was doing and when he was doing it. Besides, he might be shy. He might not be too sure that you'd say yes. Then he'd be embarrassed and wouldn't be able to leave quickly. If you'd said no to him, he would've been stuck there until Ada and Samuel decided to go home."

"I hope you're right."

"Of course I am. It makes sense when you think about it. If you were a man, would you ask a girl out if you thought she'd maybe say no?"

"I guess not. It would be embarrassing. It would crush me if I really liked the person and they said no."

"Exactly. And you'd want to walk away quickly, right?"

"*Jah,* I would."

"You see? He couldn't ask you here. From now on, it's important that you be home as much as possible just in case he stops by."

Bliss screwed up her nose as she filled the sink with hot water. "But you said he wouldn't ask me here at home."

"If he feels you'll say yes, he will."

"Yeah, you're right. I hadn't thought of that. I

haven't shown him that I liked him. He needs to know that doesn't he?"

"Just a little. Don't overdo it."

Bliss nodded. "I know what you mean."

"Good. With watching my older sisters, I'm experienced in these things. I've watched what men do when they're courting a girl, and before they are, when they're thinking about it."

"*Denke*, Cherish. I don't know what I would do without you."

Cherish took up a tea-towel. "Neither do I."

Bliss gave her a big smile, and then plunged a pile of dishes into the hot sudsy water.

On Tuesday evening, Cherish couldn't wait to find out whether her visit to the farm was on or off. When she got to Florence's house, she found a note at the door. The note told her that Florence and Carter wouldn't be back until seven that night or a little later, but they would collect her from her house at five in the morning.

Cherish was delighted and skipped all the way home. She'd already packed her bags in anticipation, and even better, Bliss had opted to stay home.

Everything was going just how she'd planned.

CHAPTER 11

AFTER MANY HOURS OF DRIVING, Cherish pressed the button of the car to lower the window. Then she stuck her head out when her farmhouse came into view.

It looked the same as ever.

She hadn't told Malachi they were coming and yet the garden looked perfectly kept and all the fences were still in good order. Despite her expecting Malachi to fail in his job, it seemed like he was looking after the place well, but she'd reserve her judgment until she inspected the animals.

As soon as Carter pulled up outside the house, Cherish shot him a quick thank you and ran to the front door.

When no one answered, Cherish pushed it open. "Malachi?"

She then turned around and saw him coming out of

the barn with a pitchfork in his hand. He'd been cleaning out the stalls. He stood the pitchfork beside the barn door and walked over to the car just as Florence and Carter were getting out. Cherish had wanted to be the first to talk to him and was disappointed. She walked over as fast as she could.

"Hello, Malachi."

He looked across at her, grinning. "Hi, Cherish. I wasn't expecting you. You didn't call to let me know you were coming."

She noticed he had a day-or-two's worth of stubble on his chin. That would not do if the elders saw that. "We thought we'd surprise you."

Carter looked at Cherish, shocked, and then said to him, "We didn't know you didn't know we were coming. Sorry about that. We can always stay at—"

"No, there's plenty of room here. It's fine. The *haus* is cleaned and the beds are made up."

"How about we take our things inside and you show Cherish the animals? She's talked of nothing else all the way," Florence said.

He laughed. "Sounds like a plan. Cherish?"

"Sure." She hurried toward him.

"I'll show you the goats first."

"Good."

"How have you been?"

"Pretty good."

"And how about your new stepfather and new stepsister? How's that working out?"

She sighed. "Up and down. I just can't wait until I'm old enough to be on my own. I'm mature enough, but I just have to wait for the years to catch up with my mind."

He laughed. "I know what you mean, I think."

"Florence is having a baby."

"Ah, I thought she might've been."

"It shows now, so good that you noticed. My two sisters have both had a boy each. My two older married sisters, that is."

"I guessed they might've been married."

She walked on pleased he was so easy to talk with. "Wilma and Levi are getting along better. It was rocky at the start, but things are better now."

He chuckled. "You call ya mother Wilma?"

"Not to her face of course. Bliss, my stepsister, was going to come here but she changed her mind at the last minute. There's a new man in town and I convinced her that he'd be perfect. I had to tell her he might change his mind and stay on in the community if he fell in love with her. She didn't like him because he was only staying here for a short time."

"Interesting. You had to convince her?"

"*Jah,* he's perfect for her."

"Really? What do you know about him?"

Cherish grimaced. "He's handsome. Not that she wants someone handsome. She said she didn't care. The main thing is she doesn't want to move away from her father. Now she's attached to Wilma too and even calls her *Mamm*. Can you imagine that?" Cherish shook her head in disgust.

"Sounds like you're a little jealous."

"What?" Cherish screeched. "Jealous of Bliss?"

He smiled at her and remained silent.

"I am not! To be jealous of someone is to want to be like them. Bliss is the last person I want to be like. Oh, that sounds mean. I don't want it to sound like that." She shoved him. "You're making me sound horrible."

He laughed as he mock-stumbled away.

She kept walking. "I've made an observation about relationships."

He caught up with her. "And what's that?"

"They're all about compromise."

"And is that a problem for you?"

"*Jah*, of course. I want to do what I want to do when I want to do it."

"That's a mouthful. Can ya say that ten times, fast?"

"Probably not. I think Dagmar had the right idea. She didn't need anyone out here on the farm."

"She died alone, childless. Is that what ya want? Don't ya want little ones runnin' 'round?"

"She wasn't alone, silly. She had all the animals. I was here when she died and hey ... that's probably just how she wanted it. She loved me and I loved her. I'll have plenty of nieces and nephews. Do I really want to compromise and do what the other person says?"

"Yeah, but there's the other side. Companionship, togetherness, love."

"They can be replaced by keeping busy."

He scratched the back of his neck. "You make it hard for a man to get close to ya, Cherish. What would a man do if he was startin' to have feelings for ya?"

She stopped in her tracks and looked up at him. She could tell he was talking about himself, and she could never be with a man who talked the way he did. It was annoying, and not proper. Again, she gave him a shove, harder than last time. "Why do you have to go and ruin everything?" She stomped away with her fists curled. What was he thinking, liking her? She was never even nice to him.

"Hey, wait up." He ran after her. "You thought I was talking about me?"

Her feet came to a halt. She turned around and looked up at him. "Weren't you?"

CHAPTER 12

HE TOOK off his hat and ran a hand through his hair. "You and I have never gotten along. You're bossy and opinionated, and you as good as said you don't want to listen to no one."

She put her hand over her heart. "That's a relief."

"*Jah*, I know. Didn't know I was that bad, but anyways, long as we're clear you're the last, the very last woman I'd ever see meself with."

"Phew! Me too. Now we can be friends again."

"Suits me just fine." He adjusted his hat. "Nothing more—ever."

"Good. Never, ever. Not in a million, gazillion—"

He grabbed her by the shoulders and turned her away from him. "Let's keep walkin' up the hill. I love it up here."

"Okay."

When they were at the top of the hill, he started

pointing out all the landmarks. She already knew them and maybe better than he did, but still, she listened. "I appreciate that you genuinely love my farm, but I have to tell you, you won't be here forever. I'll be here to take it over one day and one day soon." She shrugged her shoulders and then kept quiet. If she said too much he might leave too soon. That would ruin everything. It had been hard enough to find him to manage the farm.

"I know it. I'll love it while I'm here and *Gott* will find somewhere else for me to go when it's time."

"You don't have a plan?"

"Nope. No plans too far ahead. I have plans for the farm for while I'm here, how to make it better and such."

Remembering her talk with Florence, she said, "You've done a good job even though I haven't agreed with all your changes."

"You've agreed with nuthin' at all."

She laughed. "That's true, but now I can see that they weren't too bad."

"You have been blessed, Cherish, to be given this place. Some folk work their whole lifetime and don't get nuthin' as good as this."

A feeling of warmth flooded through her. "I have been, and I am grateful. *Mamm* was upset because she said it should've gone to all my sisters, too. What do you think about that?"

"I'd say that your aunt wanted you to have it. From what I see, she understood you. Maybe your family don't. Apart from Florence, that is. Florence and Carter are fond of you."

"Well, Florence, of course, but Carter? I'm not so sure. He puts up with me."

"That's an effort sometimes."

She gave him another shove.

"Ow." He held his arm and pretended to pout.

"I'm not that bad."

"You kind of are."

She stared into his eyes and felt a flutter in her tummy. *No!* He definitely wasn't her type. "So, what's been going on around here while I've been gone? In the community and such?"

"Same ole same ole. Nothing really. Ruth next door is still spying on me. She drives past real slow and sticks her head out of the car."

"How's your *onkel,* the bishop?"

"He's good. Nothin' different goin' on there. Nothin' changes around here."

"I bought Bliss a rabbit for her birthday that's coming up soon. I haven't broken the news to *Mamm.* She'll hate it, but I couldn't resist him."

"Wait a minute. Doesn't Bliss live with you? Where's the rabbit?"

"I should've explained. It's not her birthday yet. I bought the rabbit and someone's keeping it for me until her birthday. Then I'll collect the rabbit and give him to Bliss."

"Ah, then your mother will see how much Bliss loves the rabbit and won't be able to say no."

"Yeah. I hope it'll work out like that." Cherish looked up at the bright blue sky and stared at the fluffy clouds that were rolling by. She wondered what Adam was doing right about now. Would she forgo her future single life to eventually marry Adam? How would Adam like the farm?

"Watcha lookin' at?" Malachi asked looking skyward.

"The clouds."

"Ya figurin' out what they look like?"

"*Nee*. They all just look like clouds to me. Fluffy clouds. Puffy cotton-candy clouds. I could use some candy right now." Cherish let out a big sigh. There wouldn't be any candy around here and there were no stores close by to get any from. She should've brought some with her.

"Why are you so uptight all the time?"

"Me?"

"*Jah*."

She was shocked she'd given him that impression. "I'm not!"

His eyes opened wider. "You are."

She went to shove him again, but he ducked out of the way. "Wanna see the vegetables I'm growin'?"

"Where are they?"

"Back by the house."

"*Nee*. I want to stay here for a while. You were right,

it's nice here." She sat down right there on the top of the grassy hill.

He planted himself next to her. "Sorry about what I said."

"What part? You say a lot of things."

"The uptight thing. You don't smile much, is all."

"I do." She looked down at the grass and plucked out the longest blade. "I have a lot on my mind all the time."

"Worries?"

"Mostly. My new stepfather puts pressure on us to get jobs and then he wants us to give him all the money. Hope works six days and hands over all her pay. I only work part-time. I hold back my tips. Is that bad?" She stared at him. "Does that mean I'm dishonest?"

"Hmm. Did he say you have to give him the tips?"

"*Nee,* but only because he doesn't know about them. If I told him, he'd want them too."

His head tilted to one side. "Why does everyone have to give him money? Don't you guys have an orchard?"

"*Jah,* an apple orchard, but he's got this idea about pooling the family money. Poor Favor and Bliss can't even find jobs. I feel so sorry for them." She looked at him. "So, would you tell him about the tips if it was you?"

He stared at her. "I know what you're trying to do. You think I'm making money out of something here and not telling ya."

"*Nee* I'm not thinking that. Wait, are you?"

He jumped to his feet. "I can't believe you'd ask that. After all the hard work I do here." He marched away.

Cherish was shocked. He'd always been so mild-mannered and even-tempered. Then she realized if he left, she'd have no one to manage the place. She scrambled to her feet. "Hey wait up." He kept walking without listening. She ran after him and pulled on his arm to stop him.

He swung around to face her and folded his arms.

"I'd never accuse you of such a thing. I was talking about my own situation. I never for one moment was being tricky and talking about the farm here. I mean, my mind is not that devious, or in fact, that clever."

His face broke into a grin and then he laughed. "I gotcha."

"Was that just all an act?"

"Yeah. I was actin' like you do most of the time."

Cherish found that funny. He wasn't as stupid as he seemed. "I do not."

"Do too. You act all sulky."

"Oh. I didn't know. Do I really?"

"Yeah every time somethin' doesn't go your way. And, just so you know, everything I make out of this place goes into the books. I mightn't speak right, but I do know me numbers."

He was right about that. She was so pleased that Adam could speak nicely. Cherish laughed. "You tricked me. I thought you were truly angry. Come on, show me those vegetables. We can collect some for dinner if any are ready."

FOR DINNER THAT NIGHT, Florence made them a meal. She'd brought all the ingredients with her to make the bologna and the baked pork with apple sauce. Fresh vegetables from the farm were added and Cherish made a potato salad.

While they ate the meal, Carter asked Malachi some questions. "And what changes have you made on the farm?"

"Aargh, don't get Cherish started about that."

Carter's lips twisted in amusement. Then everyone laughed, except for Cherish.

"There's nothing wrong with wanting things to stay exactly the same. If something is working, why change it?"

"To make it better," said Malachi.

Florence said, "He hasn't made very many changes this time have you, Malachi?"

"I wouldn't be game," he answered reaching for a second helping of potato salad.

"Do you feel too isolated here?" asked Florence.

"No, I like the peace and quiet. My uncle is not very far away, and we do have the regular church gatherings.

People stop by from time to time, although, not that often."

"And how are you getting along with Ruth from next door?" asked Cherish, knowing the answer. For some reason, the old lady next door and Malachi disliked each other intensely.

"Not at all, nothing is changed there. She's always seemed set against me."

"I can't think why," said Cherish. "Maybe she doesn't like change, same as me."

"I know, right. Tell me about it. She's always watching, every time she drives past. When I wave to her, she never waves back."

Cherish tried to laugh and nearly choked on her food and ended up coughing. "Excuse me," she said and then cleared her throat.

"Last time you were doing the drainage for your orchard. How's that going?" Malachi looked between Florence and Carter.

"All finished now," Carter answered. "We're preparing the soil and the next thing we'll be doing is the planting. It'll still be years though before we have a crop of apples."

"Except for at the Jenkins' orchard," Cherish corrected him.

"Yes, we do have that. It doesn't feel the same because we're not working on that one."

"You have another orchard?" Malachi asked.

"Yes. It's on the other side of Cherish's family orchard. They have apples and cherries and a few other trees. The previous owners agreed to stay on for a year to manage the place, which suits us perfectly with the baby coming and all. Hopefully, they'll stay on another six months after that since most of that year has flown by already."

Malachi turned to Cherish, who was sitting next to him. "It's a wonder you don't want to change this place into an orchard, Cherish. It sounds like you're surrounded by fruit trees and orchards."

Cherish laid down her fork and knife, while she swallowed her mouthful. "How many times do you have to be told before it sinks in? I don't want anything changed here. There are a few fruit trees here and that's how it shall stay."

"Okay, if that's what you want."

Cherish cleared her throat. "That's true what you said. I'm sorry, I didn't mean to sound rude. I just get tense when I come here for some reason. It's a big responsibility taking over something that Dagmar loved so much. That's why I hate change, can you see that?" She stared at Malachi hoping he'd understand and see her point of view.

"It's nice to see someone care so much about something."

"I do, it's true. And I have been surrounded by apple trees all of my life. But I can take them or leave them. I'm not passionate about apples like Florence is. *Dat* loved his trees and he's passed that love down to Florence. It skipped by the rest of us."

"That's true. I do love my trees."

"I'll try not to be so beastly, Malachi. You must think I'm a horrible person. And I'm not, not really."

"I don't think that at all, Cherish."

The smirk on his face told Cherish otherwise.

Florence and Carter excused themselves and left the table right after the meal and without dessert.

"I have one more day here."

"It'd be nice if you could stay longer."

"I don't know how I'll get back here in the future. I'll probably have to wait until their baby is older and they haven't even had it yet."

"I'm sure someone else could bring you. You could hire a car."

"I will. Yes I will. That's how I came here when *Mamm* sent me here." She giggled again at how she'd been so badly behaved that Florence and her mother had sent her to Dagmar for discipline.

"You'll have to save up your tips," he said.

Cherish put her finger up to her mouth. "Shh."

They both laughed.

CHAPTER 13

THE DAY after Cherish got back from the farm, she had two shifts at the café. It was mid-afternoon, when Jainie, her work friend pulled her aside.

"CHERISH, ISN'T THAT YOUR FRIEND?" Jainie pointed at a man who had just sat down. It was Fairfax, the man Hope was in love with.

"Yes. it is. I'll take his order." She wasted no time hurrying over. "Fairfax, hello."

He looked up from the menu he'd just picked up. "Hello, Cherish. How are you doing?"

"Fine. I'm surprised to see you here."

"How's Hope?"

"I don't know. She'd already left when I woke up this morning. Didn't you take her to work?" She didn't want to let on how upset Hope was.

He looked down, and then looked back at her. "She hasn't said anything to you?"

"What's happened?" Cherish pulled out a seat and sat down. Her boss wasn't in for the afternoon, so she decided to take her break early.

"Are you allowed to talk?"

"I'm officially taking my break now. Besides, we're not busy." She turned around and caught the eye of her friend and held up ten fingers signifying she was taking a ten-minute break. "Tell me everything that's happened."

He leaned back in the chair. "There's nothing much to tell." He swallowed hard.

"We had a difference of opinion."

"When did this happen?"

"A few days ago now."

"I've been away at the farm for a couple of days. Things have been so busy that we haven't really talked."

He rubbed his chin. "She can't be missing me very much."

"I'm sure she is. I'm sure she's missing you a great deal. She's never felt like this about anyone else. She told me so."

"Is that right?"

"It is."

"I guess that's good. I think."

"Of course it's good."

"Unless …. Unless she's changed her mind."

"Why don't you just say you're sorry, and it will be better. It doesn't matter if you're in the wrong or not. Just say sorry and get back together. I know you both like each other a lot. You like her or you wouldn't be here talking to me. That's why you came here isn't it? You didn't come for the coffee. Although, it is very good coffee."

Slowly, he nodded. "It's more complicated than that, Cherish. It's not something where one of us can say sorry and then it'll be all better."

"Tell me what happen then."

He shifted in his seat. "I shouldn't say more. As long as I know she's alright."

"She is, but she's looked miserable for days and now I know why."

He searched her face. "She's really looked miserable?"

"Yes. But she just sees me as the silly younger sister, so I suppose if she's got any real problems, she would talk to Joy. She's the sensible one." Cherish gave him a big smile.

"Okay. Well it was good talking, Cherish."

"I'll get you a cup of coffee."

"It's really not necessary."

"On the house. Well, not on the house. I'm not going to steal it. If you stay and eat a slice of pie with me, I'll pay for it. And I'll keep you company while you eat. I do get a discount."

He chuckled. "Okay. I can't say no to pie."

"Who can?" She twisted in her seat and caught Jainie's eye. "Two coffees and two peach pies."

"Coming up."

Cherish turned back to Fairfax. "It won't be too much longer."

"Thanks."

She didn't want to ask him what their argument was about since he hadn't said. She'd find out later from Hope.

"Something in your stomach will make you feel better. I can't have you leave here looking miserable. You might scare potential customers away."

He laughed. "I wouldn't want to do that. How's your farm coming along?"

She sighed. "I wish it wasn't so far away. It's hard to keep an eye on it, know what I mean?"

"Hope said you had someone looking after it, but you didn't see eye-to-eye with him."

"He does what he wants. He doesn't listen to me even though I'm the owner. I suppose I do have to let him do what he wants. I'm not paying him anything. He earns his keep and keeps the profit, that's it."

"That's very fortunate for you having a farm at your age." He rearranged the salt and pepper shakers. "I always thought my folks were going to leave me the orchard. Then they up and sell it with plans to move away. Nothing left for me except a job at the orchard that your sister and Carter kindly offered me. I'm grateful for it, but there's nothing like having your own piece of dirt under your feet. Knowing that you own it. Not that I've ever had that, but I'd like to. You're lucky."

"I am. Our food should be ready now. Don't go anywhere." She got the coffees and brought them to the table while Jainie carried over the two slices of pie.

"Thanks for this, Cherish."

"You're very welcome." Cherish took a sip of coffee. "Oh, did you want cream or ice cream with that?"

"No, it's fine like this, thanks."

Cherish broke off a piece of pie and tasted it. "It's not the best I've ever had, but it's pretty good."

"Not as good as your mother makes, eh?"

"Not nearly as good, and not nearly as good as what my sisters make."

"Perhaps you and your sisters could supply the cafe here with pies and cakes?"

Cherish scoffed. "That's a sore point. We want to do things like that, but Levi says no. He wants us to have outside jobs. It's a sore point, but don't worry about it. He gives all us girls a small allowance."

"So Hope hands over the money and she only gets a small allowance?"

Cherish nodded. "That's just the way it is."

"Do all Amish families run their lives this way?"

"No. It's just Levi's way. Levi is a very different kind of person. He has funny rules." She gave a little giggle as though she didn't really care.

"I had no idea."

"I shouldn't have said anything. I've got a big mouth. Everyone says I talk too much. But I have to talk a lot sometimes. Because other people don't talk enough and if I didn't talk there would be just silence. Who wants to hear silence? No one." She popped a bite of pie into her mouth while he took a mouthful of coffee.

When she had swallowed the mouthful, she said, "I really hope you and Hope can work things out."

"Me too. Do me a favor would you?" he asked.

"What is it?"

"Don't tell her I was here."

She stared at him. How did he know that was the first thing she was going to do when she got home?

"Can't I tell her?"

"No, please don't. We both need time to work things out. Work out what we want."

"Okay, I won't tell her. It'll be hard, though. Just as well you told me not to tell her, or I would've."

"I figured that." He finished the last of his pie. "I do feel a bit better after that. Thank you for making me stay here and eat it. I needed something. I hadn't eaten in a while." He pushed his chair out. "I should go."

"And I should get back to work. I've only got half an hour to go."

"Do you want me to wait around and give you a ride home?"

"That would set a few tongues wagging if they saw

me riding in your car. Besides one of the girls is coming to fetch me."

"Ah, good."

He pulled out his wallet and Cherish put out her hand and covered it. "I said I would pay for this. There's no charge to you."

"Well, how about I leave you a tip?"

"No, not allowed."

He smiled at her, pulled out a twenty-dollar bill and left it on the table. "You can't say no to a tip."

She was opening her mouth to object but before she could speak, he'd walked out of the cafe.

When she walked out half an hour later to go home, Hope and Bliss were in the buggy waiting to collect her. It was just as well Fairfax hadn't delayed his departure. Hope might have gotten the wrong idea if she'd seen him there.

CHAPTER 14

"DOES everyone know my birthday is tomorrow?" asked Bliss as Cherish climbed into the buggy.

"Jah we do."

"We're having a special birthday dinner. We'll have Ada and Samuel, and Christina and Mark will come too. Wait, Christina and Mark have left. I forgot about that."

"I didn't. I met the man who'll be working at the saddlery store while they're gone."

The rest of the drive home, Bliss talked about her birthday, and what had happened on all her previous birthdays. To Cherish, it was all background noise while she thought about Adam. She had to get over there tomorrow and get that rabbit for Bliss.

Once the girls were home, Cherish whispered to Hope she was collecting Bliss's special birthday present. It was a perfect excuse to take the buggy.

By now Cherish knew that Adam should be at Mark and Christina's house, now that they'd left. If Adam wasn't home when she knocked on the door, she'd wait for him to get home.

She pulled up the buggy, secured the horse and then looked at the house. There was no sign of life. She walked over and knocked on the front door trying to stop her heart from beating fast.

To her surprise, Adam was there. He opened the door, smoothing down his dark honey-brown hair. It fell tangled, ending just above his shoulders. "Cherish."

"*Jah,* it's me."

He stood smiling at her for a moment.

"I've come to see the rabbit. I mean, to collect the rabbit for my stepsister."

"Come in."

She walked in past him, and into the living room where she sat on the couch.

"I hope the rabbit isn't the only reason you're here."

She was distracted, seeing all his clothes strewn about the place. He picked up one of his shirts from the back of the couch and tossed it on a chair before he sat next to her. Then she realized he was flirting with her. "What?"

"I hope you haven't come only for the rabbit. You promised to come on a buggy ride with me. Your brother left me to look after everything here and that includes me having use of his horses and his buggies."

She was smiling so much her face was aching. "I haven't forgotten, and I can show you around."

"When is your sister's birthday?"

"Tomorrow. So this is perfect timing. You did bring the rabbit, didn't you?"

"Of course I did. Would you like to see him?"

"Yes please."

"Come on." He held out his hand as he rose from the couch. She placed her hand in his and he led her to the bathroom. She giggled when she saw all the hay around the floor. Christina would've screamed to see her house in such a mess.

She bent down to have a closer look. "He's so cute. Have you named him?"

"Yeah, I told you already. His name's Bruiser."

"Oh, that's right. How could I forget that? He was the trouble-making one, wasn't he? Annoying all the other bunnies just like Bliss is always annoying us." She looked up at him, hoping he wouldn't think she was mean, but he didn't look at all shocked. "How many brothers and sisters do you have?"

"I'm the oldest of eleven. Five boys and six girls."

"Well I'm the youngest of six girls and I have an older half-sister and two older half-brothers, one of them is Mark of course, and now the latest addition is a new stepsister. That's who the rabbit is for. She was a friend of ours before her father married our mother. We do like her. I shouldn't say mean things. I'm not normally like that."

He chuckled. "I don't think you're mean. I can tell you have a lot of affection for her or you wouldn't have been thinking about her birthday so far ahead of the day. This'll be a lovely surprise for her."

"I do like her. My sisters were friends with her even before our parents married."

"Yes, you just told me that."

She swallowed hard. What he didn't know was she had been looking for an excuse to get to know him when she saw him with those rabbits. He was just the kind of man she'd been looking for. One who only saw the good in her. "I'm sure she'll love Bruiser. How do we look after him? We've never owned a rabbit before."

"As you can see, he likes hay."

"That's no problem. We have loads of hay."

"Good. If she wants to keep him in the house, she'll be pleased to know he can use a litter tray."

"That solves some problems. Yes, I think she would like to leave him in the house. When I leave home and take my dog, there will be no dogs in the house. Right now there's only my dog because Joy took hers, and now he stays around her and Isaac's caravan."

"Caravan?"

"Campervan, trailer-type of thing. That's where they're staying until they get their own house. They're saving up. They didn't like living with the rest of the family."

"It's on your property at the apple orchard?"

"Jah, that's right. Isaac can tell you all about it when you're working with him at the store."

"Okay." He rubbed his jaw. "Back up a minute. You say you have a dog in the house, and you'll be keeping Bruiser in the same house?"

"That's right."

He shook his head. "I don't think that'll work. Most rabbits are scared of dogs."

"Caramel wouldn't hurt a fly. He's timid too. He'll run from the rabbit, trust me. It'll be fine."

His eyebrows drew together. "You sure about that?"

"Jah."

"One more thing you'll have to know is that the rabbit will chew on the furniture."

"Oh."

"Their teeth never stop growing and they gnaw continually."

Cherish wished she'd known that up front. Her mother would surely have a heart attack if her furniture got chewed on. At least the dogs could be let outside, and the bird was in the cage, and the barn cats lived in the barn. In her heart, Cherish knew this wasn't going to be a good fit, but she'd already committed to it.

"So, do you think your family is ready for this little guy?" He rubbed Bruiser's furry back.

"Most definitely. He'll be a great addition to the family." At least, she knew Bliss would love him and they'd make it work somehow. "I love animals and so does Bliss. He'll be going to a good home."

"That's the main thing. The other thing is they do shed a lot."

Cherish swiped a hand through the air. "I'm used to that. Caramel sheds all year 'round. And I guess they eat fruits and vegetables?"

"That's right."

"We always have plenty on hand. And loads of apples." Cherish giggled.

"Did you hear that, Bruiser? I found a good home for you."

"I can't wait to see her face when she first lays eyes on him." Cherish was also hoping that Levi would let Bliss keep him. If he allowed her then *Mamm* would have to agree she could keep the rabbit. If not, maybe she could persuade Fairfax to look after him until another arrangement could be made. If that failed, she could take him to her farm.

"I'm sorry. Where are my manners? I should've offered you a hot drink, or a cold one."

She wanted to prolong her stay there and a hot drink would take longer to make. "I'd like coffee or maybe hot tea. Whichever one you can make best."

"That would be tea."

"Okay."

He closed the bathroom door on the rabbit. "I'm keeping him in there, so he doesn't chew all of Christina's furniture."

"Good idea. She wouldn't be happy if she came back to all her furniture destroyed. I think we could make an area for him to play outside. A big outside screened-in area. Then he can chew as much as he likes. We'd only put him in there when we're watching him, mind you, so he'll be safe from hawks and such."

"Sounds like he's going to be spoiled."

"Oh, he will be. He'll be the best cared for rabbit in the county."

He walked into the kitchen and looked in all the jars that were sitting on the countertop while Cherish sat at the table.

"What are you looking for?"

"The tea bags."

"Ach nee. You'll never find them. Christina only has tea—real tea leaves—loose leaf tea." Cherish grimaced, glad she hadn't insisted on coffee if he thought he made tea better.

"This them?" He showed her the contents of a couple canisters.

"Jah."

"How does that work? My *mamm* or my sisters always make it. Is it like instant coffee where you put them in the cup and then add hot water?"

Cherish rolled her eyes. "Sit down. I'll do it."

He grinned at her as she stood up.

"Are you really that hopeless?" she asked him.

"I'm not familiar with women's work."

"Hey, it's not women's work unless you're married. It's survival if you're not. Do you really mean to tell me you can't make a cup of hot tea?"

"Yeah, I can, with a tea bag."

"That's what I thought." Cherish filled up the teakettle and popped it onto the lit stove. "I hope you can cook, or you'll starve by the time Christina and Mark get back."

"I can fry things. Most things can be cooked in the frying pan, right?"

Cherish sighed. "I suppose that'll keep you alive."

He chuckled. "When are you coming on that buggy ride with me?"

"When do you want me to?"

"Tomorrow. I'll pick you up if you tell me where you live."

"I'm working tomorrow. You could get me when my shift's over."

"Okay. What time?"

"Oh—I'm off at two o'clock. So, who's working at the store today?"

"A friend of Mark's is working there today and tomorrow and then I start. I'm supposed to see what to do tomorrow, but it won't be long before I pick it up. It can't be hard, can it? It's just selling things and I've already learned all the products."

"I hope you're going to work hard for my brother."

He laughed. "Of course I will. And not because he's your brother and you're looking at me in that way, but because I always work hard. I'll work all day and then I'll fetch you when you finish work—except you haven't told me where yet—and we can spend all evening together."

She was then reminded that he didn't know how old she was. She'd never be allowed to stay out so late. "I'm sorry, but I can't tomorrow. It's my sister's birthday dinner. That's why I came to get Bruiser today. You could come too. Drop hints to Isaac that you're lonely and hungry and I'm sure he'll invite you along."

"You think so?"

"Of course he will. We can spend more time together if my parents think you're a friend of Isaac's."

"I am." He grinned at her.

"I know, but—" She was interrupted by the kettle whistling. "Come over here and I'll teach you something you don't know." He walked over and she proceeded to show him how to brew a pot of 'real' tea. Then she poured two cups and gave one to him. As they sat down at the kitchen table, she said, "Do you think you could do that?"

"What? Make the tea?"

"*Jah.*"

"It's easy enough. Anything's easy once you're shown what to do."

They smiled at each other as they sipped their cups of tea.

Once they finished, Cherish said, "I'll have to get home and find a place to hide Bruiser until tomorrow morning."

"Okay. I'm glad you stopped by."

She smiled at him. "I had to, to get the rabbit."

He stood up. "I'll get the cage and put it in the buggy for you. You can keep the cage too."

"Oh, I can pay for it."

"No you won't. It's an old one I wasn't using."

"Okay. Thank you. I didn't give much thought to a cage."

She followed him to the bathroom and watched how strong he was to pick up the cage effortlessly. Then she walked outside with him while he placed it in the back of her buggy.

"Thank you. Don't forget now. Be sure that Isaac invites you to dinner. It will look better than me inviting you."

He smiled at her. "I'll do my best."

"Wait. Don't go anywhere." She lifted up the buggy seat and found her tip money from today's shift. Then she spun around to face him and handed him a dollar. "There. That was our deal, wasn't it? A dollar for the rabbit."

He threw his head back and laughed. "It was indeed. Keep it." He closed her fingers around the coin.

"I insist." She opened his fingers and placed the coin in the palm of his hand.

"Okay. I shall hang onto this dollar and think of you."

She couldn't stop smiling as she turned and climbed into the buggy. "Bye, Adam. I hope I see you tomorrow night."

"Me too."

She took hold of the reins, turned the buggy around, and headed for home

Once Cherish pulled up outside her barn, she unhitched the buggy, rubbed down the horse and turned him out into the yard, and then she stared at the rabbit in the cage wondering what to do with him. Out of nowhere, a voice boomed behind her.

"What is *that?*"

She spun around, horrified to see her sour-faced mother.

CHAPTER 15

CHERISH STARED AT WILMA. She'd had no time to think of a good excuse to bring Bruiser into the household especially when she knew her mother hated animals of any sort inside the *haus*. "'*That*' is a pet bunny-rabbit. It's Bliss's birthday present."

"*Nee!*"

"He's so soft. Feel how soft he is, *Mamm*. Bliss will love him. And he'll be no problem."

"Caramel and Goldie will rip it to shreds. You mark my words. You wait and see. I can't believe how stupid and selfish you are, Cherish."

"Caramel won't. I'll introduce the two of them and see what Caramel thinks."

"It's a dog's instinct to eat them."

"Where is Bliss?"

"She's out with her *vadder*. They'll be back before the evening meal."

"Perfect. I'll see what Caramel does. I'll keep Bruiser in the cage and bring Caramel here right now."

Mamm placed her hands on her hips. "This'll be good to watch."

Cherish ran out to the yard and called for Caramel. Caramel and Goldie bounded toward her. She walked with them to the house and closed Goldie inside and grabbed Caramel's leash from the hook just outside the door. With Caramel firmly on a lead she led him to the barn where the rabbit sat in the back of the buggy.

"I've got a friend to introduce you to, Caramel. Now I want you to be nice."

Wilma scoffed. "The dog doesn't understand what you're saying."

"He might not know what I'm saying, but he knows what I mean."

"Same difference," said Wilma, now standing with hands on hips and feet spread apart, head tilted in her 'mothers know everything' look. More than anything Cherish wanted to show her mother Caramel was not going to eat the rabbit.

When Caramel saw Bruiser in his cage, he stopped and stared wide-eyed. Then he slowly moved forward with Cherish ready to pull back hard on the lead if he made a leap at the cage. What Caramel did next surprised Wilma. He put his nose down and sniffed the rabbit. The rabbit stayed still with his nose twitching. Then Bruiser moved closer and the two touched noses for just a second before then bunny leaned back and they continued to watch and smell one another.

"They like each other. See that, *Mamm*, they're not going to hurt each other at all."

"I didn't think the rabbit would hurt the dog, silly girl. I said the dog would eat the rabbit."

"Either way, it's not going to happen. I wonder if Goldie will be good too."

"Why don't you try it?"

"I will. I'll get Goldie now and leave Caramel in the *haus.*"

Wilma leaned against the side of the barn. "This I'd like to see. I'll be surprised if the other one is so good."

Once Cherish was back with Goldie and the very moment he spotted the cage, he leaped at it and Cherish could barely hold him back. "Stop it," she yelled.

Wilma stepped in and yanked the lead out of Cherish's hands. "See, I told you. Get rid of the rabbit before you break Bliss's heart."

Wilma dragged Goldie away.

Cherish looked at the terrified rabbit cowering in the corner of the cage and her heart broke. "I'm sorry, Bruiser. I didn't think this would happen. Stay there." She ran after her mother and caught up with her and Goldie. "Bad dog, that is not a wild rabbit. This is a pet rabbit, Goldie. And don't you forget it. Where are you taking him, *Mamm?*"

"I'm taking him to Joy to keep in her camper van.

The moment he's free he'll be off to find that rabbit again."

"Oh, I didn't think of that."

"There's a lot you never think about, Cherish. Like bringing the rabbit here. A rabbit is not a pet."

"But it is. I heard they make great pets. The best, even."

"Not when you have dogs!"

Now Cherish felt bad. Even Adam hadn't been pleased to hear she had dogs. The rabbit would have to stay inside at all times and away from those dogs as it would probably be terrified of dogs now from that dreadful experience. "What if we leave him in the *haus, Mamm?* You saw Caramel is fine with him."

"*Jah,* today, but what about tomorrow? If Caramel sees him hopping about it might trigger his instinct."

Cherish sighed. "I was only trying to do something nice for Bliss. She wants a pet so bad and I want her to feel she's a part of this family."

Wilma ignored her and by that time they'd reached the caravan. "Joy, open up."

Joy opened the door and looked down at Goldie. "What's he done?"

"Nothing, it's what Cherish has done. She bought a rabbit and now your dog wants to eat it. Keep him with you until we get rid of the rabbit."

"*Nee, Mamm.* It's for Bliss."

"That's *wunderbaar.* Bliss has always wanted a pet.

That's all she's talked about. Can't you let Bliss keep him, *Mamm?*"

Mamm's shoulders drooped. "Do you think so, Joy?"

"I do. Every girl needs a pet. Someone to love and to care for."

Mamm groaned. "All right." She turned to Cherish. "You make sure your dog stays away from him and I will not have any mess in my *haus*. The rabbit will have to be kept in Bliss's room."

"Done deal. And I was thinking we could make a big enclosure outside where he can play. Maybe Levi can build it for us?"

"You'll have to ask him about that."

Cherish hugged her mother. "You're the best. *Denke.*" Cherish ran all the way back to the rabbit, and somehow, she managed to carry the cage into the kitchen. Then she sat down and tried to work out where she'd hide him from Bliss until tomorrow.

Mamm WALKED into the kitchen and placed a towel over his cage.

"What's that for? He's not a bird."

"It'll quiet it down."

"He wasn't even making any noise."

"Calm it down, I meant. Now get him out of the kitchen. It's probably got germs and diseases and shouldn't be around food. I still can't believe you would do this to me."

"It's for Bliss. It's been so hard for her to adjust to this new family and that would be our way of showing her that she's accepted. We have accepted her fully and she knows that you don't like animals and that will show her how much you think of her."

"Do you think so?" asked Wilma.

"I do, and not only will it please Bliss, it will also show Levi how much you care about his only child."

"That's true. Levi has been good to us all."

Cherish remained quiet. She had nothing more to say about Levi. Nothing good, anyway.

"I'll move him upstairs to my room. Can you help me? The cage isn't too heavy."

Together they walked the cage up the stairs and into Cherish's room. Now Cherish just had to keep Bliss out of her room tonight.

OVER BREAKFAST THE NEXT MORNING, everyone gave gifts to Bliss. *Mamm* and Levi gave her a new apron and cape that *Mamm* had sewed. From the girls she got a new coffee mug, bars of scented soap and lavender shampoo.

Cherish waited until last. "I've got something special for you, Bliss."

She looked up from the table. "What is it?"

"Stay here."

Cherish ran to her room and picked up Bruiser.

"You'll get a nice new owner. I'm sure she'll love you. If not, I'll keep you for myself." She hugged Bruiser against her chest as she walked down the stairs and then she entered the kitchen.

Bliss gasped when she saw the rabbit and her bottom lip started wobbling. "Is that for me?"

Out of the corner of Cherish's eye, she saw her mother's disapproving face. Thankfully, Levi had already left the house to help a friend with something. "It's a bunny. Of course he's for you. His name's Bruiser and he's a boy."

Bliss hurried over and took him out of Cherish's arms. "Oh, I love him. *Denke,* Cherish. Oh, *Mamm,* can I keep him?"

"*Jah,* but we'll have to work out where he can stay."

Cherish hurried over to *Mamm* and kneeled beside her. "*Denke, Mamm.* Look how happy Bliss is."

"Bruiser, is that his name?" Bliss buried her face into the soft fur of the rabbit.

Mamm huffed, and whispered, "You should've asked me first before you brought it here. You should know better, Cherish. We're trying to keep rabbits off the property. Why would you bring one in?"

"He's a pet. He's not a wild rabbit." She giggled. "Is that what you thought, *Mamm?*"

"He is cute," Hope said stroking the rabbit.

"And it is my birthday present, *Mamm,*" said Bliss to her stepmother.

"We'll have to see what your *vadder* says about this,

Bliss. More than likely he'll say it should be Sunday dinner." *Mamm* giggled, but no one else did. "Is that why you bought him, Cherish?" *Mamm* added, trying to make a joke.

"He's a pet."

"And what does Caramel think of him today?" *Mamm* asked.

"Caramel is fine with him. He ignores him. Goldie won't be a problem if he stays out of the house."

Mamm turned to Bliss. "Do you know how to look after the thing, Bliss?"

"I could learn."

"As long as there is no mess in the *haus,* your *vadder* will probably agree for you to keep him. He has the last word on the matter."

Bliss and Cherish exchanged grins. They were more than halfway to keeping him. Cherish knew *Mamm* would've already told him about the rabbit last night, and he'd not stopped her from giving him to Bliss.

CHAPTER 16

CHERISH WAS CLEANING her bedroom while thinking about Adam. She hoped Isaac would invite him to dinner. Favor and Bliss had gone into town looking for work yet again.

Then Cherish realized her mother was alone in the kitchen and that she hadn't had much alone time with her recently, so she headed down the stairs.

"What are you doing, *Mamm?*" she asked when she walked into the kitchen.

Wilma looked up at her. "I'm cooking Bliss's favorite meal and it's Levi's, too. He's doing a lot for this family. It's not easy for him to look after us all."

Cherish bit her tongue. They'd managed by themselves for so long, what was hard about it? "That's nice, so you two are getting along better?"

"*Jah.* He was trying too hard to be the head over us

and now I think he knows he doesn't need to be so harsh."

"That's good." Cherish popped a piece of cold cooked meat into her mouth, surprised her mother hadn't scolded her for asking such a thing. "What is Bliss and Levi's favorite meal?"

"Potato pie."

"Good. I like that too." Out of the corner of her eye, Cherish saw the bunny hop into the room. She knew her mother wouldn't be happy about it being around food.

Just when she was figuring out that she needed to do something to distract her mother, and then put the rabbit back upstairs, he started gnawing on the table leg.

"What's that noise?" Wilma looked around.

"What noise? I don't hear anything."

Wilma looked down and screamed, jumped back and knocked the bowl of peeled potatoes onto the floor. The pottery bowl broke into a thousand pieces. Then she wailed. "It's ruined. Dinner's ruined." She crouched down and lunged at the bunny and caught him. She carried him out of the room.

Cherish knew her mother was going to do something awful. "I'll take him. Give him to me." Cherish chased her trying to get the rabbit from her.

Wilma ignored her, holding Bruiser out of her reach. Then she opened the front door, put him down and wedged herself in the doorway so Cherish couldn't get to him, and then moved him right out the door with her foot.

Cherish screamed. "Stop!" With an almighty shove, she pushed her mother out of the way and tried to grab Bruiser, but he was frightened by all the fuss and took off, bounding. Both Cherish's knees were scraped as she landed on the dirt. She looked back at her mother as she pushed herself to her feet. "How could you? He's a pet bunny, not a wild one."

"There's no difference, you silly girl."

"I hope I can get him back before the dogs see him." She knew Caramel and Goldie were out playing together somewhere as usual.

As she ran from the house, Wilma called after her. "It was a silly thing to give Bliss anyway. We'll just tell her he got out and ran away, okay?"

"I won't say that." Cherish yelled over her shoulder as she ran. Of all the horrible things her mother had ever done, this was the worst. Having no idea which way Bruiser had gone when he'd moved past the barn, she thought it best to locate the dogs.

She was relieved when she saw the dogs with Joy near Joy and Isaac's caravan. "Joy, grab the dogs and hold them." Joy looked up at her, shocked, and then Caramel bounded toward her. She ran to him, grabbed his collar and ran with him to Joy. "Bruiser's got out and I've got to get him."

"I'll keep the dogs here. Go."

Cherish hurried off, darting this way and that unsure of where to go. All she could do was criss-cross over the orchard and hope she could find him somewhere.

FLORENCE WASN'T FEELING TOO good. She was tired these days with the *boppli* coming soon. It was normal to become tired, she'd been told, but it didn't stop her from worrying that something could be wrong with either her or the baby. Being her first, she wasn't sure what to expect.

She was deliberating whether to take Spot for a walk when he jumped off the couch and headed over to her and placed his head on her knee. "You want your walk, don't you, boy?"

He stared up at her with his big brown eyes.

"Come on then. We'll just go at a slow pace. That's all I can manage today. I'm sure I'll feel better in the fresh air."

Carter had gone to town to load up with groceries and then she had him go to the specialty store to get her favorite ice-cream. She'd had cravings for two things since she'd been pregnant. Pistachio ice-cream and caramel. It was the caramel inside the chocolate candies that she wanted and only one particular brand satisfied those cravings. Even though she knew there wasn't any particular nutritional value to be had in those foods, and they were mostly all sugar, she did nothing to resist the urges. Her nutritional intake was plenty good enough to keep her growing baby well nourished.

Florence leaned down and snapped a lead to Spot's collar and together they headed out of the house. Once she was outside in the late afternoon sun she felt better. The cold air that nipped at her cheeks helped to revive her tired body.

Every time she looked at the flat land it reminded her of how far off having a full running orchard was. It tugged at her heart that Levi was allowing her family orchard to run down. If only she could've taken over and run the place, but that was something that Wilma wouldn't hear of once Florence left their home and eloped with Carter.

As Florence wandered down the fence line, she recalled how she'd once secretly hoped Levi would run the orchard into the ground and then she'd buy it from them cheaply. It wasn't nice to benefit at the expense of others, so she'd squashed those thoughts from her mind completely.

Tomorrow, Eric Brosley was meeting with her to discuss the next step with the orchard and that was the soil preparation. He'd been invaluable with his orchard knowledge. He'd been a friend of her father's and he reminded her so much of him. If her father had been alive, he would've welcomed Carter into the family. His heart had been as big as his smile.

Suddenly a rabbit jumped out in front of them giving both Florence and Spot a start. She knew Spot would give chase, so she held on tight. She wasn't wrong. Spot bounded into the air and then pulled on the leash so speedily that it burned through Florence's hands in a split second, knocking Florence off her feet. She landed on the ground with a thud.

The baby!

She'd landed on her front. Tears rolled down her face as she sat up. Spot was in the distance still chasing after the zigzagging rabbit. Florence pushed herself to her feet and made her way back to the house. Just as she pushed the door open, a pain stabbed at her stomach. If she had the baby now, he'd never survive. It was far too early. If only she had stayed inside and not gone for a walk. She picked up the cell phone that Carter insisted on her having and called him.

"Carter, I fell hard. I'm worried about the baby."

"I'm two minutes away."

"Hurry." She ended the call and lowered herself to the couch and sobbed.

This couldn't be happening.

A few minutes later, Carter burst through the door. "What happened, are you okay?"

She tried to repeat what had happened but couldn't talk through her crying. "I fell," was all she could say.

And, "I'm worried about the baby." He kneeled down in front of her and held her hand. She calmed enough to speak clearly. "Spot saw a rabbit. He chased it. I don't know where he is. I fell hard. The baby." Tears rolled down her face.

"I'll call 911."

AFTER AN HOUR OF SEARCHING, Cherish didn't know what to do. She'd gone all over the orchard looking in every possible place the rabbit might hide. When she heard the siren of an ambulance, she ignored it at first until it got closer.

Florence and Carter! They might've seen the rabbit.

She ran to their house. When she got past the last row of trees and headed down to the dividing fence, she saw the paramedics heading into the house. She bunched up her dress in one hand, slipped through the fence and set off running. One of them was in trouble.

Breathlessly, she burst through their front door to see the paramedics talking to Florence. Carter stood close looking worried.

"What is it, Carter? What's going on?"

Carter grabbed her by her shoulders, nearly picked her up and talked to her at the front door. "Florence fell over hard on the ground and then got pains. We're worried about the baby. They're going to take her to the hospital to get checked over further."

"Shall I go with her?"

"No. It's fine. Thanks anyway."

"How did she fall?"

He glanced over at Spot who was sitting on the couch looking guilty. "Spot pulled her over. He saw a rabbit and wanted to chase it."

Bruiser!

Cherish's blood ran cold and she sank to her knees on the floor. It was all her fault.

"It's okay, Cherish. It's just a precaution. I'm sure everything will be all right." Carter crouched beside her. "There's nothing to worry about."

She looked into his kind eyes. Now was not the time to tell him the rabbit belonged to Bliss, or that she was the one who had brought the rabbit to the house. "I should go, then. Let me know if you need me. You've got the number of the phone in the barn?"

"Sure have. I'll call to give you an update as soon as we know anything."

"Where did it happen?" Cherish stood and so did Carter.

"She said she was down at the fence-line. She normally goes for a walk in the afternoon."

"I know. She's always done that."

Cherish glanced out the door. "Um … which way did the rabbit go?"

He frowned at her. "She didn't say."

"Don't worry. I hope she'll be okay. We'll pray for her."

"Thank you. I'll let her know you're praying."

Cherish nodded, and then looked back at Florence who was still busy with the paramedics. "I'll go now." She hurried out the door. When she was a distance from the house, she kicked the dirt with her lace-up boots. "Great! Just great! Chased by a dog and then no one knows which way he went. He could be anywhere by now. What will I tell Bliss? What will I tell Adam if he comes to dinner tonight? And poor Florence. I'll never forgive myself if something bad happens."

She ran down the fence-line looking everywhere for the rabbit. Half an hour later, she realized she was faced with an impossible task and headed home.

When she walked in the front door, she heard Wilma humming in the kitchen. This was no time for her mother to be in a good mood. She hadn't been in a good one for years, so why start now? Cherish stomped into the kitchen not bothered by her dirty boots.

Wilma turned around to face her. "Well?"

Cherish planted her fists on her hips. "Well! Do you want to know what trouble you've caused by being so mean to Bruiser?"

Wilma chortled. "Don't be silly."

"Our dogs didn't chase him, but Carter and Florence's dog chased him while Florence was out walking. Florence ended up falling and now … there are paramedics there seeing if she's okay."

Wilma slapped her hand over her mouth in shock. "Will she be all right?"

"They're taking her to the hospital." She wanted to add that it was because of Wilma letting Bruiser out of the house.

Wilma rushed to sit down, and tears spilled down her cheeks. "This is dreadful, just awful."

Immediately, Cherish was glad she hadn't said more. She sat down next to her mother and wrapped her arms around her neck. "It's my fault for buying the rabbit. I don't know why I did."

Wilma patted Cherish's arm, but kept on crying. "I've never liked animals in the *haus,* and you girls never listen."

"Sorry, *Mamm.* How about I finish off the cooking?"

"It's done. Anyway, Levi likes me to do it."

"I'll do the cleaning up, and get things ready for the visitors." Cherish bounded to her feet and whizzed around the kitchen putting the dirty dishes in the sink ready for washing and putting all the food items away. Next, she filled the sink with sudsy hot water, covering the dishes to let them soak for easy washing later. Then she sat down with her mother again.

"Do you think she'll be all right?"

"I do. Carter said it was just a ... hmm ... he said it was just a precaution. I think that's the word he used."

"Then why is she going to the hospital at all? There must be some question mark."

A lump formed in Cherish's throat. Why couldn't she wake up and start this day all over again? "We have to believe and pray."

"Jah, we'll do that." Wilma grabbed Cherish's hands and closed her eyes.

Cherish closed her eyes tightly too and prayed for the safety of Carter and Florence's baby. At the end of her silent prayer, she asked *Gott* to look after Bruiser, too, and bring him safely home. She hoped it was okay to pray for an animal.

Wilma opened her eyes. "What became of the rabbit?"

Cherish shrugged her shoulders. "I don't know. He's gone."

"What will we say to Bliss?"

"We'll have to tell her that he got away. Maybe he'll come back."

"She won't be happy."

"I'll tell her if you want, *Mamm?"*

Wilma shook her head. *"Nee,* I'll tell her."

"All this happened when you were singing and happy. I mean, humming. I haven't heard you hum in ages." It was since before *Dat* died, in fact, but Cherish didn't want to make her mother feel worse by mentioning him. They'd loved each other very much, and now she was saddled with Levi. It must've been depressing for her and now there was no way out.

"Perhaps I should lie down."

"Nee, don't let this upset you too much. Things happen, accidents happen. We've just prayed so let us believe for the best outcome." Cherish bounded to her

feet. "Stay there and I'll make you a cup of coffee and fix you a snack."

"Your *vadder* always looked on the bright side. You take after him, Cherish. You're always so merry."

Cherish laughed on the inside. No one had called her merry before, but she was pleased her mother thought she was similar to her father. Perhaps they'd both been thinking about him just now. He was never far from Cherish's mind.

"Mrs. Braithwaite, your blood pressure is high."

"She's had a shock too," Carter told Dr. White, the female doctor from Emergency. "As well as falling hard."

The doctor then listened to the baby's heartbeat. "Sounds nice and healthy. You should check back with your own doctor in a day or two. Until then I suggest complete bed rest."

"Stay in bed? Until when?"

"At least until you get in to see your doctor. Let's see what's going on with the baby, shall we? I'll order an ultrasound."

"Good. I was due for one of those soon."

Shortly after the doctor left, a portable ultrasound machine was wheeled into the room. After Florence's tummy was squirted with gel, the technician ran the scanner over. Carter and Florence watched the fuzzy figure moving around.

"That's our baby," Carter said in awe.

Florence couldn't speak. If the baby was moving, did that mean it was okay?

"Everything looks fine. The heart's beating nicely." The technician pointed it out on the monitor. "There's no cause for concern."

"The sharp pains?" Florence asked.

A nurse walked in at that moment and answered the question. "Your blood work is fine, and everything looks normal apart from your raised blood pressure. The pains could be from something entirely unrelated. Possibly even something you ate."

"I have been eating some odd things lately. Something could've upset me."

"So, our baby's totally okay?" Carter asked.

The technician nodded. "Your baby's fine."

Carter and Florence looked at the image on the monitor of the ultrasound. "Do you want to know what you're having?" the technician asked.

Florence looked at Carter. "Do we?"

"Do you?" he shot back.

"I think I do."

He smiled at her and gave the technician a nod.

"Yes, we want to know," Florence told her.

"You're having a girl."

Carter grabbed Florence's hand. "We're having a

girl. I wanted a girl. I thought I didn't care either way, but now I hear that, it's just what I wanted."

Florence laughed. "Me too, but I didn't want to say. I'm so used to girls after all my sisters. I helped raise all of them." All Florence felt was relief. The day had been a disaster, but now everything was perfect. She could manage bed rest if that was needed. Most of her days had been spent resting anyway.

CHAPTER 17

As soon as Carter and Florence were home, Carter made Florence go to bed. "I'll be fine on the couch. I'll walk up to bed at night."

"No. You heard the doctor. Bed rest. It's nearly bedtime anyway." He pulled down the covers and she got in.

"I'm still in my clothes."

"You can change out of them later. I'll bring you up some dinner."

"Thank you."

He leaned over and kissed her on the forehead. "I'll have to call Cherish. She was very concerned, and she'll be waiting by the phone."

"I saw her come in, but I couldn't talk to her."

WHEN BLISS, Levi, and Favor came home, Cherish ran out to meet them and to tell Bliss the news about Bruiser. She was trying to save her mother from the awful task of telling her

She stood next to the buggy and waited for Bliss to get out. "Bliss, I have some bad news."

"What is it? Are we late?"

Cherish shook her head. "It's nothing like that. It's Bruiser, he got out and ran away."

Bliss's mouth dropped open and her whole body sagged. *"Nee."*

"It's true and I'm not joking."

"How did he get out?" Favor asked, joining them.

"He just got out. I tried to get him before the dogs did, but he was too quick. I didn't see where he went but I think he might have gone to Florence's next door."

Everyone looked at her, and Levi joined them.

Cherish continued. "That's not all. Florence's dog saw a rabbit, chased it and pulled her over. She had to go to the hospital."

"Oh no!" Bliss started sobbing.

"I should call Ada and Samuel and tell them not to come tonight."

"Jah, Dat. I couldn't enjoy it now. Besides I have to look for Bruiser."

Now, Cherish's day had just gotten worse. If the birthday dinner was canceled that meant that Adam wasn't coming for sure.

"Let's go, Bliss. I'll grab the flashlight." Favor ran into the barn.

"Okay," Bliss said blinking back tears.

"I'll fix the horse. You two go."

When Favor came out of the barn with the flashlight, the two girls hurried into the darkness of the orchard. It was just on dark, not a good time to find the bunny.

Just when Cherish had finished rubbing down the horse, the phone in the barn rang out. Cherish hurried to answer it, hoping it was Carter. "Hello?"

"Hi, Cherish it's Carter."

"How is she?" Cherish felt sick to the stomach. She'd never forgive herself if something happened to Florence or the baby.

"She's fine, and the baby is fine. It was just as well we went in when we did, though. Turns out she's got high blood pressure and she needs complete bed rest."

"How did she get that? Was that because of the fall?"

"Totally unrelated."

"So, it was good that she fell?"

Carter laughed. "Well, not really, but it did work to our advantage, I guess."

"Can I come and see her tomorrow?"

"I'm sure she'd like that."

"Thanks for calling me."

"Of course. Bye, Cherish."

Cherish ended the call feeling much better. Now if only they could find that rabbit!

She put the horse in the stall and hurried inside to tell her mother the news.

THAT NIGHT over a very late dinner, everyone was talking about the rabbit and Florence. As much as Hope was upset about Florence not being well and the rabbit going missing, she couldn't get her mind off Fairfax. He hadn't been in touch with her at all and she was heartbroken. Half of her wanted to forget him. If he was seriously interested in her and loved her as much as she loved him, how could he *not* contact her?

Cherish had her mind on Adam. Had Isaac invited him to the dinner only to have to cancel the dinner? She hoped Adam wasn't offended. What if he thought someone didn't want him there?

Bliss felt awful, and guilty as well, about her rabbit being the cause of Florence's fall. Her birthday was ruined. She never remembered having a good birthday anyway. Maybe next year she'd finally have a better one.

Favor sat at the dinner table, upset and sad for Florence, but she wasn't happy that Bliss got everything she wanted and so did Cherish. All she wanted was for a pen pal to stay for a week or two. She'd been asking for years and she was continually ignored. When would anyone care about her? She was always overlooked. If only she'd been the youngest, or the oldest. Both of them got things easier. Being anywhere in the middle of the family was tough. One year, when she had been too upset to have her birthday dinner with guests over, no one had even suggested a make-up birthday dinner on another night like they'd suggested to Bliss. It was just canceled. No one even gave it a second thought.

CHAPTER 18

THE NEXT DAY OVER BREAKFAST, the Baker girls were deciding what clothes they'd make for Florence and Carter's baby, and then Wilma suggested they make some food to take to Florence since she was on bed rest.

"I'll bake them an apple pie," said *Mamm*. "But you girls will have to take it to her."

"Aw, come with us." Favor pouted at their mother.

"*Nee*. We're not really talking."

"Can you wait for me to come home before you go?" Hope asked.

"Sure," Favor said. "Well, maybe."

"And can someone drive me to and from work tomorrow? I'd just like a little rest from cycling all the time," Hope said.

When Levi frowned at her like he so often did, she

added, "Since I'm the only one with a fulltime job, I didn't think anyone would mind doing that for me."

Slowly, he rubbed his beard. "I think someone could take you and collect you, Hope."

"*Gut, Denke,* Levi. Tell Florence I said hello, will you, Cherish? I'll see her when I finish work in the afternoon."

"Sure."

Hope kept eating her cereal. She'd not eaten much since she and Fairfax hadn't been talking.

Cherish was quiet. Today, she had some plans of her own. She knew Adam would be in the saddlery store today and she had a good excuse to see him.

JOY WAS the one who drove Hope to work. From the time they got out of the gate, Hope couldn't keep her words in any longer and she unburdened herself about Fairfax, telling Joy absolutely everything. "So, what do you think?" she asked when Joy wasn't saying too much.

"I'm not sure."

Hope's heart sank. Maybe she shouldn't have talked to Joy. Love had come so easy for her. She hadn't even been looking. "I know you don't approve because he's an *Englisher*."

"I don't, Hope. You're right about that. Look at Florence."

"Well, she is in love with Carter, but I don't want to leave the community. Fairfax said he'd join."

"Jah, but he didn't do it. He might've been stringing you along all the time and when things got too close, he knew he had to end things."

Hope held back tears. It was probably right, what Joy was saying, but she still didn't want to believe it. "I had dreamed of a future with him." She sniffed.

"I know it's hard, but better that it ends now before you got too involved with him, and he led you astray."

Hope bit down hard on the inside of her mouth. She didn't want to arrive at work in tears.

"You'll feel better soon, after some time passes."

"I don't think I'll ever love anyone else."

"You will and it'll be the right man. Fairfax was obviously the wrong man. If he was the right one, he would've talked to the bishop like he said he would. The right man wouldn't have you feeling like you are now."

"Jah, you're right, Joy. I wish I'd never got close to him. It was a silly thing to do. He made promises and …"

"Don't even think about him now. He might've been genuine when he told you those things, but it's a big thing for him to leave everything he knows and all his family to join us."

"I know. It would be. Now I feel so wretched." Hope blew out a deep breath.

"You'll be okay. I'll fetch you at two when you finish."

Hope looked up to see they were already at the bed and breakfast where she worked. *"Denke,* Joy." Hope jumped down from the buggy wishing her circumstances could be more like Joy's. Everything just worked out for Joy, and she was happily married to Isaac.

When Hope walked into the building, she looked in the book to see what needed to be done. Fairfax's aunt —her boss—walked out.

"Good morning, Hope."

"Hello, Mrs. Jenkins."

"Are you ill, Hope?"

Hope looked up from the book. "No."

"You look pale." She walked closer. "Have you been crying?"

"No, I'm okay." She did her best to control her emotions, but one tear escaped. It trickled down her cheek and she wiped it away.

"I don't think so. What's happened?"

"It's my older sister. She had a fall and now she's had to go on bed rest. She's pregnant you see. I'm visiting her after work."

"Oh dear, I hope she'll be okay. Are you alright to work or would you like to take the day off?"

"No. I'd prefer to work. It'll keep my mind off things. I'm okay with visiting her when I finish today."

"Call me Jane, please, when no one's around." Jane

smiled. "You're a good worker, Hope. I'm glad Fairfax recommended you."

Once again, Hope had to bite down on her tongue at the mention of Fairfax. "Thank you, Mrs. Jenkins— um, Jane. I'm pleased that you're pleased with me."

Jane laughed. "Take it easy today. Make sure you take all your allotted breaks."

"I will."

Jane went to walk off and then they both looked at the white pickup truck pulling into the driveway. "Ah, speak of the devil. It's Fairfax."

Hope wasn't in the mood to face him. Besides, it was working hours. "I'd better start on room 3."

"Don't you want to see Fairfax?"

"No. We had a bit of a falling out and … I can't face him today. Not with being upset over my sister. I just … don't want to talk."

"You go, then, and I'll deal with Fairfax."

"Thanks." She grabbed her cleaning cart and headed off to get room 3 cleaned before the next lot of guests arrived. As soon as she got to the room, she pushed the cart in, left the door ajar and listened. She heard Fairfax's aunt tell a lie. Jane told Fairfax she wasn't in today.

"How is she?" Fairfax asked.

"She's fine. Why?"

"Aw, nothing. I'll stop by later, Aunt Jane."

"Did you want to have a cup of coffee with me and tell me why you're looking so distraught?"

"Some other time."

"What is it?"

"My folks and I are having a disagreement."

"What is it this time?"

"It's about … it's kind of … It's hard to explain."

"Oh."

Hope clutched at her throat. He'd told them he wanted to join, and they disapproved. It couldn't be anything else. At least now she knew what was going on. She wasn't left wondering. She listened at the door until she heard him leave, and then she went about her work doing the best she could to put him out of her mind. It seemed he wasn't going to stand up to his parents.

Over the course of the day, she saw Jane several times and no mention was made of what Fairfax had told her.

As much as Hope wanted to put Fairfax out of her mind, it was hard. Everywhere she looked, she saw happy couples. A honeymoon couple had arrived to stay in room 3. She saw the way they looked at each other, and she wanted that for herself. Fairfax had looked at her like that. Another happy couple was holding hands when they arrived back from a morning of sight-seeing.

CHERISH PRETENDED she had a shift at the café that she'd forgotten about. Levi allowed her to take one of the buggies when she told him she'd only be working for two hours filling in for one of her friends who had a dental appointment. She didn't mean to tell such outrageous lies, but as soon as she told a small one, it just got bigger and bigger and soon she'd told Levi a complicated story. It was surprising that he believed it. He'd looked at her without blinking when she was telling the story and made her even more nervous.

As bad as she felt for telling tall tales, it was worth it to see Adam again. Once they were engaged, she might even confess her deception to Levi and if enough time had passed, they might even laugh about it.

The horse's hooves clip-clopped along the road at a steady pace as she dreamed of how Adam would smile when he saw her walking into the store. There had certainly been an attraction between the two of them when they met at the mud sale. When she told him the sad story of how Bruiser had escaped, he'd offer her sympathy. Maybe if she could summon a tear or two, he'd even put his arm around her.

When she arrived at the saddlery store, she secured her horse, gave him a pat, and then breezed in through the front door. At first, she didn't see Adam, so she rang the bell on the counter. He came out of the back room, and when he saw her, his face fell.

Cherish was taken aback. He didn't look pleased to see her at all. Had some girl told him untrue stories about her? If only Bliss hadn't canceled her birthday party. "Hello, Adam."

"Cherish. I heard about Bruiser."

"I know. I'm so sad." She looked up into his face and what she saw didn't resemble sympathy. Then he folded his arms.

"Isaac told me a dog chased him."

"I know, a dog. Not one of my dogs."

"Cherish, you told me you'd keep Bruiser away from dogs and keep him in the house. I trusted you. What was he doing on the next-door property where a dog could get him?"

Isaac walked out of the back room and she looked over at him. He couldn't have known Adam would react in this way.

"Do you think it's my fault?"

"Yes."

This was terrible. She wanted a man who could see no wrong in her. It would sound worse to blame her mother. Besides, he might not even believe her.

"Rabbits deserve to be cared for properly. I only give my rabbits to responsible people. You had me believing you were worthy of a rabbit."

Cherish's jaw dropped. "I am. How can I help it if he ran away and didn't come back? It's not my fault."

"And, your poor sister has suffered too, when the dog pulled her over. That never would've happened …"

Isaac stepped forward. "Now just a minute, Adam. I know everyone's upset about the rabbit and what happened, but Cherish is very good to animals. She cares for her dog very well, has done so for years."

"*Denke*, Isaac."

"I'm sorry, Cherish. I'm going to have to ask you to leave. I can't look at you right now."

Isaac stepped forward and put his arm around Cherish's shoulder. "Come on. I'll walk you out."

Before they got to the door, a tear trickled down Cherish's cheek. She had thought Adam might be her future husband, but now he hated her.

When they got to the buggy, Isaac said, "I'm sorry. I should've kept my big mouth shut, but he was coming to Bliss birthday and I had to give him a reason that it was canceled."

"That's okay, Isaac. You stood up for me. That means a lot."

"Will you be—"

"I'll be fine." She climbed up into the buggy and headed for home. One thing she'd been right about, she had gotten an arm around her shoulder. Unfortunately, it was only her brother-in-law's. Also, she had shed a tear, but not a fake one.

WHEN THE WORKDAY came to an end, Hope hurried out to Bliss who was waiting instead of Joy. She climbed up into the buggy. "I'm so glad to get away from work. *Denke* for coming to get me. Are we going straight home?"

"*Jah,* and then we'll go to see Florence. The others

didn't wait. They already saw her, but we can see her again."

"*Denke*, Bliss. I hope we find Bruiser while we're walking to see her."

"I hope so, too, but I've been looking most of the day and haven't seen him."

Hope felt bad for her. "You're coming with me to see Florence?"

"*Jah*, if that's okay? I saw her earlier, but I'll come back again."

"How is she?"

"Big." Bliss laughed. "She's okay. She said she'll be fine."

"Good. I've been so worried. Fairfax came to see me today. His aunt told him I was out." She sighed.

"Why didn't you talk with him?"

"*Nee*. I don't need to hear bad news. I already know he was coming to end things properly. I overheard him say he was having an argument with his parents and I'm sure it was about me. He probably asked them what they thought about him joining us and they didn't like it. If he was a real man, he wouldn't have needed to ask them."

"Not everyone can make the commitment to *Gott* and the community that we do."

"I know that, but he said he was going to speak with the bishop and then he didn't. Why say something if he wasn't going to go ahead with it?"

"Because he loves you and he really, really wanted to do it, but then he couldn't."

Hope turned and looked at the passing fields. She was out of step with everything. The mid-afternoon sun drenched the fields in golden light, and yet inside she was miserable. Weeks ago, she'd felt that same light from within, but now all there was in its place was wretchedness and tormenting darkness snatching at her insides and twisting them. "I know I shouldn't be so upset. Joy would say I should trust, and I know I should, but that doesn't stop me from being sad."

"I don't know what to say to make you feel better."

Hope sighed. "Just talking helps. Thanks for listening."

Bliss turned the horse into their driveway. After they unhitched the buggy, they walked into the house to see Wilma.

"*Mamm*, we're going to see Florence now. Do you want to come?" Bliss asked.

"*Nee*. You know the answer to that before you ask it."

Since Levi wasn't around to influence her mother, Hope stepped forward. "Don't you want to see her? She'd be so pleased to see you."

Mamm stared back into Hope's eyes. "I know she would, but things are just awkward now with Carter."

"I understand, I guess."

"Shall we tell her you said hello, *Mamm?*" Bliss asked.

"Better than that. I've made up a food basket. With her bedridden, she won't be able to cook. I've made a few meals to keep them going." Wilma moved over and took hold of a basket.

"*Ach,* Hope. It'll be so heavy."

"We can each carry a handle. That's nice of you, *Mamm*. Florence will appreciate it and so will Carter."

"It's my way of doing something for them. Hurry along and come back soon so you can help me with the evening meal."

Hope was pleased her mother had done something nice for Florence. It was a sign of hope that the two women might talk again one day. Of course, the gulf between them had become deeper since Florence had left the community. Things would never be the same as they once were.

Bliss and Hope set off through the orchard, each holding one side of the basket. "I hope Bruiser comes back one day. Do you think he's all right, Hope?"

"I'm sure he's out there somewhere having fun. I'm sure he knows his way home."

"But it wasn't his home for that long. How would he have known it was his forever home? He wasn't here for much over a day."

"We've prayed for *Gott* to look after him and bring him home. Now all we have to do is wait." When Hope saw a smile on Bliss's face, she shot another prayer heavenward that the bunny would find his way back.

CHAPTER 19

THE TWO GIRLS traded sides and rested several times between the two houses, but they still had aching arms and hands by the time they got to Florence's cottage. Carter's car wasn't there, but they knew Florence would be in bed. They set the basket down and knocked on the door.

"Come in," they heard Florence say.

Hope pushed the door open and they dragged the basket in. Once they shut the door behind them, they saw Florence resting on the couch covered in blankets. Hope ran to her and put her arms around her neck. "Are you better?"

"The funny thing is I'm feeling fine. When I fell, I had sharp pains, but they've gone now. They tell me I have high blood pressure."

Bliss walked over and stood close. "Wilma cooked you and Carter some meals."

A smile lit up Florence's face. "She did?"

Bliss continued, "*Jah,* she did, and she said she's not coming because the whole thing is awkward now with Carter and her, and you too."

"That was very nice of her to cook for us."

"I'll put them in the kitchen."

"Thank you, Bliss."

Hope sat on the floor, on the rug beside Florence. "We've all been so worried about you." She whispered, "Even *Mamm.* She cried when she found out you were at the hospital. She does care."

"I know."

Bliss came out. "I put everything in the fridge. You could put some in the freezer."

"Thanks, Bliss. Carter can sort it out when he gets home. Thank Wilma for me, would you?"

"Sure. Where's Carter?"

"He's in town choosing yarn and patterns for baby outfits. He'll be back soon."

Bliss laughed. "You trust him to do that?"

"Not really, but how could he get something like that wrong? I wrote down exactly what I wanted and what colors."

"What about Spot?" asked Bliss.

"He's around somewhere. He must be upstairs. He's taken to sleeping in the bedroom. Ever since the warmer weather arrived, the upstairs is nicer."

"Florence, I'm sorry about what happened to you. It

was my fault because the rabbit was probably the one I got for my birthday. He got out and ran away."

"It's not your fault, Bliss. Things like this aren't anyone's fault. They just happen."

Bliss opened her mouth to speak again, so Hope chimed in and asked Florence, "Do you want us to put the fire on for you?"

"Ah, that'd be nice. It gets cold quickly in the afternoons."

Bliss pushed past Hope. "I'll do it."

"*Denke.* Well, if Bliss is doing that, can I get you something to drink or eat?"

Florence laughed. "I couldn't fit anything in. All I'm doing is eating and sitting or eating and lying down."

"Must be exhausting," joked Hope.

Florence nodded to the knitting on the coffee table. "I've been keeping myself busy knitting an outfit for the baby. It's all I had to knit."

"The *boppli's* due in early August, right?"

"Yes. It seems such a long way off, but I suppose it will go quickly. That's another reason to keep myself busy."

"Upstairs you've got your bedroom and a study, right?"

"Yes. The baby will stay with us and when she's old enough, Carter will divide his office. It used to be two rooms."

Bliss turned around from the fire she was blowing on. "Wait. Did you say 'she?'"

Florence giggled. "Whoops. I wasn't going to tell anyone. Yes, it's a girl."

"*Mamm* will be so pleased. She's got two grandsons and now she'll have a granddaughter."

Hope put her arms around Florence's shoulders ever so carefully. "I'm so happy for you. Everything has turned out *wunderbaar*."

"It's not the life I thought I'd have, but I am happy. The happiest I've ever been."

Bliss warmed her back by the fire that was now alight. "Can we tell people?"

"I guess so since I opened my big mouth."

"You haven't seen that rabbit again have you?"

Hope stared at Bliss not believing she was talking about the rabbit.

"No. I've been in bed or on the couch, nowhere else."

"I miss him." Bliss frowned and her bottom lip wobbled like she was going to cry.

"He didn't hurt the rabbit. He didn't even catch the rabbit. Don't worry, Bliss."

"I'm so sorry, Florence. It's all my fault because it was my rabbit."

"*Nee*, don't be silly. It happened for a reason. I found out about my high blood pressure. If the rabbit hadn't been there, I would never have known. That can be a dangerous situation for a pregnant woman."

"Just like *Dat* used to say, all things work together for good," Hope said.

Florence nodded.

Hope pushed herself to her feet. "We've got to get back to help with the evening meal. I'm pleased you and the baby are fine."

Florence smiled. "Me too."

Bliss pushed the fire screen in front of the fire and then bid Florence goodbye before she and Hope collected the empty basket from the kitchen.

Once they were away from the house, Bliss asked Hope, "Do you think she blames me for her fall?"

"*Nee* not at all."

"I hope not. I feel bad. He was my rabbit."

"He was and still is. He'll come back. I know it in my heart."

"*Dat's* never let me have a pet after *Mamm* died. This was the first one, and I only had him for such a short time."

"I'm sure he'll be back."

"I don't know. I hope so."

They reached the fence and Hope held the wires apart so Bliss could slip through first. Bliss passed through the fence and then held the wires for Hope.

When they got home, Bliss ran into the house ahead of Hope. "*Mamm*, she loved the food and she said to thank you, and she's having a girl!"

Hope stood in the doorway of the kitchen with her mouth open. Florence was *her* sister and she wanted to be the one to tell *Mamm* Florence was having a girl.

"A girl?" Wilma asked.

"Jah."

Wilma held onto the kitchen counter all the way while she walked to the table and then she sat down.

Hope sat opposite her. "You'll be three times a *gross-mammi* and you're having your first grand *dochder."*

Wilma smiled and put her hand over her mouth. "I'll pray for the *boppli.* She might come back to us one day even if Florence never does."

Levi walked into the kitchen. "What's for dinner?"

"Dat, Florence is having a girl," Bliss blurted out nearly bouncing up and down.

Levi stopped and placed his hands on his hips. "Is that so?"

"Jah, it is. Hope and I were just there."

He walked further into the kitchen. "So, what's for dinner, Wilma?"

Wilma stood up. "We're having a pot roast."

"Again? We had one last week."

"That's right," Wilma said, "and we're having another one tonight."

"Make me a cup of hot tea, would you?" With that, Levi left the room.

Even though he had improved in some areas, he still liked to order their mother about, Hope noticed.

"I'll make the tea, *Mamm,"* said Bliss.

"Denke, and Hope and I will start on the vegetables."

CHAPTER 20

OVER DINNER THAT NIGHT, Levi proved he wasn't through with grumbling. First it was the meat that was tough, and then it was the girls' employment, or more correctly, the lack thereof. "I'm not sure you girls are looking hard enough for jobs. What do you do out there all day? If you're messing about, you could be home helping your *mudder*."

"We're looking for jobs," insisted Favor.

"Is that right?"

Favor nodded and Bliss agreed.

"From now on I want you to write down every place you inquire at. I might have to check on you and ask them if they've seen you. I want you both to come home only after you've been to five places."

Hope noticed that Bliss and Favor exchanged glances.

"Sure," said Favor. "We'll be happy to do that and then you'll know we're not making up stories."

"I'll give you a blank-paged book tonight after you finish the dinner wash up. Then I'll check it every evening."

Everyone was quiet throughout the remainder of the dinner and nothing else was said, not even about Florence. No one wanted to give Levi an opportunity for more grumbling.

Hope stared at her mother and wondered if she regretted marrying Levi. Had she desperately clutched at Levi as someone who would solve all her problems and look after the orchard after Florence left home? It seemed so, but she couldn't judge her mother. She was just as sad for herself, the way she'd pinned all her hopes on an *Englisher*. She really should've known better.

Fairfax hadn't even asked her to leave the community to be with him, not seriously, although her quick no hadn't left room for discussion. He'd just chickened out and backed out, worrying more about what his parents thought than about what Hope thought.

Now she'd have to marry someone else. Everything had been so much easier for Mercy because Ada had matched her with Stephen, and then it was easier still for Honor because she married Stephen's older brother, Jonathon. Perhaps she'd end up with Stephen and Jonathon's younger brother if no one else showed up for her.

Hope soon noticed she was the only one left sitting at the table. "I'm washing," said Bliss.

"Nee, I will," said Favor.

The girls' bickering went back and forth until the pair made a decision. It was the same routine every night.

Once the washing up was done and the kitchen spotless, everyone settled down in the living room for the nightly Bible reading.

"Tonight, we'll take a look at slothfulness." Levi shot Favor and Bliss a look. They were the only two of the girls left at home who had no employment. He opened his large black leather-bound Bible, while everyone was quiet, listening. "Second Thessalonians. 'For even when we were with you, this we commanded you, that if any would not work, neither should he eat.'" He wasn't subtle at all when he looked back up and stared at the two girls again.

"We are trying, Levi," Favor said. "We're not making it up. We want to work too. We don't want to keep going around asking for work."

"Try harder. The Lord will provide if the heart is willing." Levi chuckled.

Hope noticed Favor getting agitated and wanted to help her. "I'll ask my boss if she knows of any of her friends looking for staff. She might know some other business owners. She went to a council meeting the other night that was for business people."

He stared at Hope. "Why are you only thinking of this now? Don't you want to help your sisters?"

"I do. I just didn't think of it. I'm sorry."

"It'll benefit the whole family."

Hope held her tongue. She was tempted to suggest they open a stall like they used to operate. For some reason, he was dead set against the idea.

OVER AT FLORENCE and Carter's house on the next-door property a very different conversation was going on.

"I've been hesitating to mention this because I know you love this house and everything, but with the baby coming ..."

Florence smiled at Carter. "I know what you're going to say, and I've been expecting you to bring it up again. You want to build a new house here, but I do love this cottage."

"This is the best place to build a house, or we could build it closer to the road."

"Between here and the road?"

"Yes. We'll soon outgrow this place. We already have, really. I don't think this old cottage should be built onto. We'll leave it as a guest house. We should be living in something better, more modern, more suitable for a family with children."

"Children? I'm not having twins. I hope. We only

saw one on the ultrasound. This place will see us through a few more years, and like you said, we'll divide the office into a nursery soonish." They had plans of the baby staying in their room for at least the first few weeks.

"I think we should start making plans, though. I'll talk to an architect friend of mine and he can design something. It doesn't have to happen overnight, but I do think we need to make plans for the future."

Slowly, Florence nodded. "I suppose that's best. And I'm glad you didn't suggest leaving the property entirely since I was born in the house next door."

"Were you? Right at home?"

She nodded.

"I didn't know that."

"We were all born in that house. My two older brothers and my six half-sisters. And you know how I feel about the orchard, and how being close to it makes me feel happy."

"Whatever makes you happy makes me happy." He took hold of her and she looked into his beautiful eyes. She couldn't have imagined a more perfect man. It was a real love match. It wasn't a love match that made sense, but somehow together they *did* make sense.

"I suppose it's a good idea to make plans."

"Good. I'm glad you agree. When I bought this place, I never thought I'd be married and living here." He ran a hand over his short cropped dark hair. "I never saw myself as married at all, let alone being a father."

"I had half given up on finding love, but I didn't think about it too much. Not until Mercy got married." She shook her head. "It was a weird feeling with her being so much younger. I really felt that time had slipped by and it was too late. Then you came along."

"Yes. I came along and whisked you off your feet."

She giggled. "I wouldn't say that."

"No, you tried to resist my charms."

"The truth was, I didn't see your charms for a long time."

He laughed. "I wore you down until you realized I was the only man for you."

"Something like that, and now we're pregnant." She felt tears stinging behind her eyes. Finally, she was happy. Good things were happening, and she wasn't merely watching them happen to someone else.

"We'll have six," he said.

"Six babies? You said you'd be happy with two or three."

"To start with." His eyes twinkled. "The more the merrier, I say."

Florence laughed. "Let's start with one and see how that goes."

CHAPTER 21

A FEW MONTHS ON, Florence was frustrated. Her doctor had kept her on bed rest and now she was fed up. She looked over at Carter who was sitting at the end of the couch with her feet on his lap, reading the newspaper. "I just feel so fat and useless."

Carter looked up and laughed. "You're having a baby. You're not fat, and even if you were, that's not a bad thing. And useless? Never."

"I had it in my head that we'd shop for baby furniture and now that's out of the question. We're having a girl and it would've been nice if we could get some pink things for her. Time's running out. We're only weeks away."

"We can go shopping."

"Not if the doctor doesn't let me move around."

"We can shop for everything online and have it delivered." He picked up his laptop and sat on the floor beside her and wedged his computer between them. He googled some nearby baby stores, and then clicked on one of them. "Here we go. We can buy everything from diapers, and clothes to cribs to playpens."

"That's wonderful."

"Order what you want, and I'll put it on our credit card when you get to the end."

"Sit up here and let's look at it together."

"Give me half an hour to work upstairs. I've just got to reply to some emails and then I'm all yours."

"Okay. I'll do some browsing."

When Carter had folded up his newspaper and walked upstairs, Florence clicked through all the baby clothes, imagining everything they'd need. She'd never dreamed that she'd buy all her baby's clothes from a store, let alone an online store.

IT WAS JUST after lunch on Saturday afternoon, and Hope had arrived home from her usual day at work, where she started early and finished early. Cherish had been throwing a stick for the dogs and trying to teach them to return it. All they kept doing was running away with one dog at either end of the stick. Cherish left them to fight over the stick and walked over to Hope who was now unhitching the buggy. Then she noticed Hope looked as though she'd been crying. "What's wrong?"

Hope looked up at her and shielded her eyes from the afternoon sun. "Nothing."

"You haven't been yourself for days. What is it? Is it something to do with Levi?"

She huffed as she undid the horse's harness. "I wish it was as simple as that."

"Okay, it must be Fairfax then."

Hope looked at Cherish and nodded. "That's right. Things are over between us. Over before they even began."

"They did begin. He was driving you to and from work, so you saw him twice a day and that was nearly every day. And you're working for his aunt at the job that he got you."

"I know. I still am working for his aunt. That really has nothing to do with anything." Hope continued unhitching the buggy while Cherish looked on.

"Exactly what is the problem. Tell me, I might be able to help."

"Help me rub-down Bailey and I'll tell you."

Cherish grabbed the old towels they kept for the horses and gave one to Hope and kept one for herself. While they rubbed Bailey all over, Hope talked.

"He told me he was going to talked to the bishop about joining us and then he didn't. I feel like such a fool."

"That's great, isn't it?"

"Wait until I finish telling you. That was months ago and then he didn't do anything at all. The next time we talked about it, he said he was talking to his parents about it. I basically told him to forget the whole thing."

"Why would you do a silly thing like that?"

"He's a grown man. Why would he need to ask his parents? Sounds like he's double-minded, and not sure about me. What do his parents have to do with it? He's a grown man, isn't he?"

"He's is, but hasn't he got the right to speak to his parents about a life-changing decision about his life?"

Hope shrugged. "That makes sense when you put it like that, but I just want him to be so madly in love with me that he just wants to be with me no matter what."

"*Jah*, well, sounds romantic and everything like that, but maybe a person who warms up so quickly could cool down just as fast. The slow-burning love might be longer-lasting, like a longer slow-burning candle with a flickering flame that burns brighter and longer."

"When did you become so wise, Cherish?"

"What do you mean? I've always been this way."

"The other thing is his folks obviously don't approve of me and I know that for a fact from what I overheard Fairfax say to his aunt."

"Why wouldn't they approve? Do they even know you?"

"*Nee*. We were keeping things secret. Except I told you girls. His parents must have told him it was a bad idea. It would be the same, probably, as if we were to leave. If *Mamm* said we shouldn't leave the community for a man, we would be less likely to do it."

"Well, not me if I had my mind made up about something."

"*Nee*, not you, but most people."

"What are you going to do about it?"

"There's nothing I can do about it."

"Of course you can do something."

Hope slumped herself down onto a hay bale. "You know the bishop wouldn't want him to join if the only reason was for me. The relationship was probably doomed from the start. I should've resisted my feelings for him."

"I see what you mean, it's a hard one."

"I'll pray about it and just wait to see what happens. If it's God's will, he will come back to me."

"That's right. And I'll help you pray about it too."

"*Denke*, Cherish."

Cherish sat next to her on the same bale and patted Hope's arm. Maybe her sister was willing to leave things be but Cherish was a doer.

She didn't see the point of sitting back and watching things play out. Maybe God wanted someone to do something and maybe she had this talk with Hope because God wanted her to go and talk to Fairfax's parents. Cherish thought back to the time she'd met Fairfax's mother. She was nice. So, what would be the harm in talking to her again and telling her how wonderful Hope was and how suited she was to Fairfax? Although, she'd have to keep that idea from Hope. "What can I do to make you feel better, Hope?"

"My chores for a week."

Cherish was shocked. "You spat that out pretty quick."

Hope laughed. "I'm only joking. It was something you'd say."

"*Jah,* you're right about that. 'Make the most of every opportunity,' that is my motto most of the time."

"That's a bit tough."

"I'll do it for you. I'll do all your chores for a week."

"Will you really? You don't have to."

"I'll do it if you smile."

Hope gave her a big smile. "*Denke,* Cherish. That's thoughtful. I don't have that many chores to do since I work six days. Levi's let me off most of them. Would you really do that for me?"

"*Nee.* It's probably best if I don't. It'll only give you more time to think about Fairfax and more time to be miserable. Best to keep yourself busy." Cherish rose to her feet. "Let's go inside."

Hope rolled her eyes. "I knew it was too good to be true."

"I'm doing you a favor. Maybe you should do *my* chores for a week to keep busy."

Bliss appeared at the barn door. "Hey, what are you two doing?"

"Talking about you," said Cherish.

"Me?"

"Cherish is only joking. We were talking about..."

"About Hope's job. I asked if Mrs. What's-her-name can give me a job there and she said they're full up. Isn't that right, Hope?"

"They are full up, it's true."

"Denke for asking anyway. *Dat* is still getting worked up about Favor and me not having a job."

"Let's go inside," said Cherish. "It's getting cold out here."

IT WAS mid-morning the next day when Cherish seized the opportunity to talk with Mrs. Jenkins, Fairfax's mother. Cherish found her with one of her horses, lunging him in a small round yard.

She stopped when she saw Cherish approaching.

"Hello, Mrs—"

"Hello. Cherish, isn't it, from next door?"

"That's right. I'm here to talk to you about your son, if you don't mind."

She dropped the lead she was holding onto and met Cherish at the fence. "You're here to see me about Fairfax?"

"Yes."

"What's it about?"

"I know he's talked to you about my sister, and him wanting to join our community. And I just wanted to tell you why it's a good idea."

The woman's thin eyebrows drew together causing distinct vertical lines in her forehead. "He wants to join your community? Are we talking about my Fairfax?"

"Yes, I only know one Fairfax."

"Who is your sister?"

"Hope is my sister."

When Mrs. Fairfax kept frowning, Cherish felt a fool. Fairfax hadn't mentioned anything to her. "Oh no, I just made a big mistake. I'm sorry. I shouldn't have come, and I shouldn't have …. Oh no. I've probably made things ten times worse for Hope."

"Tell me more."

Cherish took a step back, then turned and walked and then started running. All the while she heard Mrs. Jenkins asking her to come back, but she couldn't. There was nothing to say. Then she reached the drive-way, still running, and the worst thing possible happened. Fairfax's pickup truck turned onto the same driveway. He stopped the truck and the window lowered. "Cherish, what happened? Is Hope alright?"

Suddenly, she stopped running. "Yes, don't worry. You didn't see me here. Forget I was over here. Forget I ever said anything to your mother."

He opened the truck door and got out. "What?"

She turned and ran again, running and running along the road until Fairfax and his truck were out of sight.

What a fool she'd just made of herself, and a fool of Hope, and probably a fool of the community. Fairfax didn't even care enough about Hope to have the discussion with his parents that he said he would. She walked a little until she got her breath back, and then ran slowly the rest of the way home.

It would be best never to tell Hope that she had talked to him and, if God was on her side, Hope would never find out. If Hope found out, she would never forgive her for being so silly. Finally, she reached the place where her driveway met the road, and walked up to the house.

Why hadn't she let things be? When she got into the house, she ran up into her bedroom, closed the door and flung herself on the bed.

She felt awful for Hope, she felt just as bad as when Adam said he couldn't look at her. Why were men such hard work?

Had Fairfax ever loved Hope? Or had he been just playing with her—laughing at her behind her back?

CHAPTER 22

FLORENCE GOT up from the couch to walk upstairs and was gripped by a sudden pain. "I think the baby's coming. This one was stronger." She'd been having weak contractions for the last two weeks, and she had been told they weren't labor pains.

Carter hurried to her side. "Are you sure? It's still a couple of weeks out."

She was just about to say of course she wasn't sure about anything when she was flooded with warm. "Oh! My waters just broke."

"We're having a baby." He held her arm. "Sit down."

"I think I'm supposed to walk around." She sat anyway without really thinking.

"You're still on bed rest."

"I think labor trumps bed rest."

He rubbed his head, looking flustered. "I should get you to the hospital."

"No, I think there's plenty of time. They won't want me to come in too early."

"I don't care about what they want. I'm not taking any chances."

That sounded good to Florence. "I've got the bag in the closet upstairs. It's packed, ready to go. I'll need a towel and a change of clothes." She stood up and looked at the wet couch. It had been a bad idea to sit down.

Carter ran up the stairs.

When he came down with the bag in hand, she was engulfed by a large contraction, more painful than the last. She did her best to breathe like she'd been practicing. Once it was over, she held her stomach. "I hope they don't get any worse than that."

Something told Florence they would.

AT 3:15 the following morning, after five hours of labor, Florence was handed a crying baby girl. All the trauma of the last few hours was the last thing on her mind as she held her baby against her. The small body was wet and sticky, and the umbilical cord was still attached. They'd been told skin-to-skin bonding was the best for a newborn and Florence wanted to do everything right. Carter looked over her shoulder, and then kissed Florence on her forehead. "She's beautiful. Good job, Mama."

"She's the most beautiful thing I've ever seen in my life. We made her."

The baby stopped crying.

"Who does she look like?" Carter asked.

Florence wondered if she looked like the mother that she never remembered. All she had were a few photographs of her. "She certainly doesn't look like my father or Aunt Dagmar. I can't say. Does she look like any of your baby photos? I think she does a little."

"I don't know. We'll have to wait until she's older."

"Perhaps she looks like herself." Florence touched her daughter's hand and the baby wrapped her fist around her mother's finger and held it tight. "Look, she's holding onto me."

"She knows who you are and doesn't want to let you go," Carter said.

"I won't ever let her go. I want her to have the best life ever."

"And that's what she shall have. Whatever she wants. Without being spoiled, of course."

When it was time, the midwife instructed Carter to cut the cord and then the baby was weighed. She was six pounds and five ounces. Then the baby was quickly bathed, diapered and wrapped tightly, and given back to Florence.

"Hello, little girl," Carter said, peering over Florence's shoulder. Then the baby moved her head as though looking where his voice had come from. "Look how strong she is. She's only just born, and she can turn her head."

"She is strong," Florence agreed.

"I'll have to call everyone I know and tell them she's arrived. Tell them I'm a dad and you're a mom."

"There's no rush. You hold her for a while. Phone calls can wait til sunrise, anyway."

He carefully took the baby from her and held her close. Tears of joy fell from Florence's eyes, and Carter's, too. It was such an amazing sight to see their baby cradled in her father's large arms. There was such love in the room.

CHAPTER 23

HOPE WAS GETTING ready to ride to work. She'd wheeled her bike out of the barn when she heard the phone start ringing. Without wasting time, she leaned her bike against the wall, and ran to answer it before it stopped.

"Hello, this is Bakers' Apple Orchard."

"This is Carter. Who's this?"

Hope knew the baby wasn't due yet. "It's Hope. Is everything okay?"

"Better than okay. We have a baby."

Hope let out a yell. "Already?"

"Yes. We have a perfectly healthy baby girl and she came in at six pounds five ounces."

"Oh, I'm so happy for you both. How long will she be in the hospital for?"

"I'm not sure. I don't know. Probably a day or two."

"Can you let us know? We'd all love to see Florence

and the baby as soon as they get out. We won't stay long, we just want to see the baby."

"I understand. I'll call you when the baby comes home. And you can arrange a time with Florence."

"Thanks so much for telling us Carter. I'll tell the others. They'll all be so happy."

"Good. Thanks, Hope."

"Oh, wait. What did you call her?"

"We haven't gotten that far yet."

Hope giggled. "I'm sure you and Florence will think of something wonderful."

"I hope so. There are too many choices. Bye, Hope."

"Bye, Carter. Give our love to Florence and the baby." She hung up the phone's receiver, ran out of the barn and burst through the front door of the house.

"She's had the baby. A girl, just over six pounds and they don't have a name for her yet."

Favor ran out of the kitchen. "When was she born?"

"Just now, I think, they're still at the hospital. Carter's going to call us when she gets home so we can go and see her. Where's *Mamm?*"

"Kitchen."

Hope ran to her mother. *"Mamm*, did you hear?"

"The whole county heard your loud voice." Her mother grabbed the counter as if she was going to fall.

"Are you alright, *Mamm?*" Bliss asked.

"I am. I'm happy for them."

All the girls were in the kitchen except Cherish, who hadn't gotten out of bed yet.

Hope wasn't going to stick around, she had to get to work.

Cherish heard what Hope said from her bedroom upstairs. She ran down the stairs just as Hope was moving out the front door. She hurried into the kitchen to see her mother seated, and Bliss and Favor sitting either side of her, as though something was wrong with her.

"I don't think I've ever been any more excited. Florence has a baby. I can't wait to see her. This is your first granddaughter, *Mamm!*"

Bliss said, *"Mamm* is a bit dizzy or something."

"Oh, is it the shock?"

"I don't know what it is. It's definitely good news and the birth went well, and the baby is healthy. It's a blessing from *Gott*. If only Florence had stayed in the community."

Cherish kept quiet. To her, there was no point saying, 'if only this, and, if only that.' Things were the way they were, and that was the end of it. There was no point in wishing things were different.

"I wonder when we can take over all the things we've made for the baby," Bliss said.

"Did they have the baby in the hospital?" *Mamm* asked.

"Jah, they did," Favor told her.

Wilma put her fingertips up to her cheek. "You'll have to take our things over soon because the baby will need a blanket."

"*Jah* and what better blanket to use than one you crocheted for them, *Mamm?*"

Wilma smiled at Bliss, but what Bliss had said turned Cherish's stomach. She made it so obvious she wanted *Mamm* to like her.

"I do hope she likes it."

"Of course she will. Who wouldn't like something that you've taken your special time and effort making, something beautiful out of love? There is no doubt about it."

Cherish glared at Bliss. She was so obvious it was laughable.

"That's right, I agree. I can't wait to see her face when you give it to her, *Mamm.*" Cherish knew her mother had no intention of seeing Florence as much as she'd want to see her baby.

"*Ach nee.* I won't go to see her. You girls can."

"Why not? Because of the community?" Cherish asked. "But Carter didn't leave the community, because he was never in the community."

"It's not that, Cherish. Things are difficult now."

"But can't we start anew? With the new *boppli,* and all?"

"*Nee.* She made her choice. Her *vadder* would've been so upset to see her waste her life the way she's doing. If I go to see her, she'll think nothing of what she's done, leaving *Gott* the way that she has.

"That's right, *Mamm.* You're doing the right thing."

The hairs on the back of Cherish's neck raised

again at the way her stepsister agreed with her mother. Why did Bliss think she needed to add her two cents worth?

All she was doing was trying to get into *Mamm's* good graces and perhaps even trying to become her favorite.

IT WAS on Friday evening that Carter called the Baker household to tell them that they were home from the hospital and the girls could visit after midday on Saturday.

With Hope at work, Favor, Joy, Bliss and Cherish gathered all the baby clothes they'd made along with the blanket that Wilma had crocheted and headed off on foot to the cottage.

The girls started off walking, but then each one started walking faster, and then Cherish ran past them. "I'm going to be first to the fence."

"*Nee*, you're not," said Bliss. "I'll race you."

Cherish ran faster leaving the other girls way behind. Bliss gave up and waited for the others to catch up. Once she reached the fence, Cherish slipped through it with ease and then waited for the rest of them. "I won," she said when they got to the fence. "I'm the fastest and the best runner."

No one said anything. Cherish held the wires of the fence apart for them all to get through. When they looked up at the cottage, Carter was there with the door open and he waved to them.

"There's Carter. He sees us," said Bliss, waving.

"We can all see that with our own eyes," said Cherish.

"Stop being mean to Bliss," Favor whispered to Cherish.

"I'm not. That's the way I always speak. She knows that, don't you, Bliss?"

"*Jah.* You talk like that all the time. I'm not offended by it."

"Good, and neither should you be."

Cherish couldn't help herself. She left her sisters and ran all the way to the house. With one leap she jumped up onto the porch and flung her arms around Carter. "Congratulations, Daddy. Where's the baby? Can we see her?"

He laughed and slowly removed her arms. "Of course. Right in there on the couch. And thanks."

Cherish walked past him, and saw Florence sitting on the couch with a small pink-wrapped bundle in her arms.

She gasped and hurried to Florence's side to get the first look at her baby niece.

"She's so pink, and look at those cheeks. And look at you, Florence. You look *wunderbaar*. The best I've ever seen you."

"I don't know why. I haven't had much sleep. This little one only seems to sleep for an hour at a time."

Then the other girls joined them and greeted Florence and got their first looks at the new baby.

"What is her name?" asked Bliss.

"We don't have one yet. All we know is we don't want to call her after anyone we know. We want her to have her own unique name."

"You better hurry and think of something," said Favor. "I have so many pen pals. You might like one of their names. There's Ruthie, Janie, Adelle, Phillipa, June—"

Bliss nudged Favor in the ribs. "Hey, she just said she didn't want to name her after anyone, least of all your pen pals, okay?"

Favor's mouth turned down at the corners and she uttered an apology.

"It's okay, Favor. Thanks for your help. Something will come to us and it'll be just right."

"We've all brought gifts," said Joy. "Shall we open them for you, or do you want to put the baby down? You can give her to me." Joy giggled.

"Nice try, Joy, but I think I should hold the baby first," said Cherish.

"Why you?" asked Florence, looking amused.

Cherish opened her mouth and then hesitated. Finally, she said, "Because I'm the closest in age to her."

"It took a while to think of that one." Carter laughed as he shut the front door behind them. "Florence has made you some afternoon tea if you'd all like to move into the kitchen."

"Aw, you didn't have to go to all that trouble, Florence," said Bliss.

"Carter did it, but I told him what to do."

They giggled. When they got to the kitchen they saw soda, and funnel cakes along with pies that had to have been from one of the local Amish bakeries.

"Missing home, are you?" asked Favor.

"This is my home now. With Carter and our baby."

"Of course it is," said Cherish moving to sit down in the seat next to Florence.

"Don't listen to Favor."

"Why don't we open the presents now before we eat?" Joy asked.

"I'm sorry, Cherish, but I'll give the baby to Joy to hold first, because she's the oldest, and then she can pass the baby to the next oldest."

"Unfair," said Cherish. "I'll be the last."

Joy giggled as she hurried to Florence to take the baby into her arms. "Your time will come, Cherish. The Bible says the first shall be last, and the last shall be first."

"Good. Finally things will turn out right for me."

Everyone giggled.

Cherish passed over the first present. Florence opened it carefully, starting at the corners and peeling off the tape. Everyone watched and waited patiently.

A look of delight spread across her face when she

pulled out the beautifully crocheted blanket. It was cream flecked with fine blue stitches, and lightweight. Perfect to keep a baby warm. *"Mamm* made this."

"How did you know?" asked Bliss.

"Because she's the only one I know who can do this quality of work, so fine, so beautiful. It's more than beautiful, it's perfect." Florence rubbed her face against it. "So soft. Thank her for me, will you?"

"Why don't you thank her yourself?" asked Cherish.

"Things didn't work out too well last time we spoke. She knows where I live if she wants to see us. Unfortunately, it's up to her."

"Anyway, pass the next present, Cherish," Joy said.

"Wait a minute. Where's Hope?"

"She's at work until two this afternoon."

"Oh. Can she come over after that?"

"I don't know if she's coming straight home, but if she is I'll come back with her," said Bliss.

"Thank you."

CHAPTER 24

THAT AFTERNOON, Hope didn't go straight home. She was missing Fairfax again. She went close to his house hoping to catch sight of him, wheeling her bike along the orchard by the fence line closest to his property. After waiting twenty minutes, there had been no sight of him.

When she gave up and started heading home, movement in the nearby trees caught her eye. She stared and couldn't believe what she saw. It was Fairfax.

He seemed just as shocked to see her.

She leaned her bike against a tree and walked to him.

"What are you doing here?" he asked.

"It's my family's orchard. What are *you* doing here?"

He grinned at her. "I mean what are you doing *here*, so close to my place?"

"Looking for you."

"Me too. I was heading to your house to speak with you."

"You were?" That meant he didn't care if Wilma or Levi saw him. That had to be a good sign. "Why did you take so long to come back?"

"You told me I had to be sure. It's a big decision and now I'm sure."

Still, she wasn't going to give her heart just yet. "When are you going to talk to the bishop?"

He chuckled. "Done."

Her mouth dropped open. "You mean, you've already talked to the bishop about joining us?"

"I did it. And you didn't prepare me for all the questions he was going to ask." He wagged a finger at her.

She giggled. "I thought I told you there would be a lot."

"He asked me about you."

"Me?"

"That's right. Someone must've said something."

"I don't know who … It was probably my sisters."

"It could've been."

She took a step closer. "What did he say?"

"I have to stay with a family for a few months, and then take instructions, and get baptized."

"What do you think about all that?"

He took a big deep breath. "I think … I better tell my parents."

"You haven't told them anything yet?"

He chuckled. "No, but they know I don't want to go

to Florida with them. I'm going to stay now. I know what I want."

She held her breath.

"I want you." He reached out his hand and she reached forward and took it.

"You do?"

"Yes, I do." He pulled her into his arms, and then whispered in her ear. "I thought I had lost you."

"Never. Thank you for coming back."

"Thank you for taking me back."

They held onto each other tightly.

"So the bishop didn't mind about me, about you dating me?"

"I didn't say that. We are not allowed to spend too much time together. We can't actually date until I'm further along in my journey."

"I thought that would happen. I don't mind. I'll wait."

He laughed. "You'd better."

"Who are you staying with?"

"I don't know yet and it doesn't matter. I'm going to do anything, go through any hard work they give me. I'll even stay on a dairy farm."

"I've heard that's hard work."

"I reckon it would be."

"Right now, this is the happiest moment I've ever had in my life."

He took hold of both her hands and kissed them.

"We'll have so many moments, Hope, much better moments than this."

Hope was smiling at him when, from the corner of her eye, she saw something white in the distance. "Oh! It's Bruiser!"

He turned to look where she was staring. "What?"

"It's Bliss's pet rabbit. He went missing." She followed Bruiser, trying not to spook him. When she got closer, she crouched down and called out to him. He hopped close to her and she gently grabbed hold of him. "I was so worried that we lost you forever." As the bunny snuggled into her arms, she looked over at Fairfax. "Come home with me? I have to get him to Bliss."

"Sure. I'll bring your bike."

"Ach, I forgot all about that."

As they walked back through the orchard, Hope knew all her prayers had been answered. God had even answered her prayer about Bliss's rabbit.

"Do you think your folks will try to stop you from joining?" Hope couldn't take another disappointment.

He chuckled. "No, they're not like that. They might be a little shocked, but they'll get used to the idea."

"Good."

"Don't worry, Hope, I've made up my mind. That's what is right for me, and that's what I'm going to do. Then we can be together. Will you marry me one day, Hope? As soon as we're allowed?"

She smiled. "I will, Fairfax."

He stopped and put the bike on the ground. "Come here."

She walked into his open arms and he encircled them about her and the rabbit she was holding. Then Bruiser wiggled and jumped to the ground and hopped away.

"Quick, get him," shouted Hope.

Fairfax took a flying leap and grabbed him. "We'd better get him to your sister as soon as we can."

They kept walking, now with Fairfax holding the rabbit and Hope wheeling the bike. When the house came into view, Hope said, "I hope she's home."

"I should head back now."

"No, come in and tell them the good news."

"I don't think I'm ready for that yet. That's no reflection on what I feel for you. It's just that I'm too nervous to meet your mother."

"You've already met her and Levi when you bought Levi's horse. The one that was really Wilma's."

"Pretended to buy the horse, you mean, on behalf of Florence and Carter," he corrected her. "That in itself makes things more difficult. My first interaction with them was one of deception."

"I know, but you were doing it with the best intentions. None of us could believe that Levi was selling him. He'd given Wilbur to *Mamm* as a gift before they were married."

"I know that. All the same, do you know what I mean? It still makes me feel bad."

"I do."

"I'd rather get to meet them slowly. Besides, if I meet them now it's more or less saying that we are a couple and as far as the bishop's concerned and everybody else in the community, we need to be friends first, right?"

"I guess so. I'm just excited." They smiled at one another.

"Me too. Should I wait for you at the road in the morning?"

"Yes, please."

He leaned forward and gave her a quick kiss on the cheek and then passed her the rabbit. "I'll wheel your bike to the barn and then I'll get out of here."

"Thank you."

They went their separate ways, and now her broken heart was mended. The door of the house was open, and she walked through and closed it behind her with her foot.

Bliss came hurrying out and took Bruiser out of her arms. "Where did you find him?"

"In the orchard."

"*Denke,* Hope. I can't believe he's back!" Bliss hurried into the kitchen yelling for *Mamm*.

Hope followed wondering how her mother would react.

Wilma stared at the rabbit with her mouth turned down at the corners. "Oh, you've got it back."

"*Jah,* and I'm so pleased. Look at him, *Mamm*."

"Nice, now get it out of the kitchen. You don't want to get him near the food."

"Oh, I think he's put on weight."

"Bliss, please get it out of the kitchen. I don't want germs to get in the soup. Those animals are full of germs and diseases."

Bliss looked at Wilma, shocked.

Hope stepped forward and said to Bliss, "Let's put him in his little hutch in your room, shall we?"

As they walked out of the kitchen, they heard *Mamm* mutter, "Cherish will be the death of me one day."

Bliss looked at Hope. "What did Cherish do?"

"She gave you Bruiser."

"*Jah,* she did. I'm so glad."

"Me too," said Hope. "He's a lovely pet for you to have, Bliss."

Mamm stomped out of the kitchen. "Bliss, get the rabbit out of my sight before I turn him into Saturday stew. Hope, take over from me in the kitchen." She undid her cooking apron and handed it to Hope, and then headed out the front door, shutting it firmly behind her.

Hope ran to the door and opened it. "Where are you going, *Mamm?*"

"I'm doing something I should've done a long time ago."

Bliss and Hope stood there staring at one another.

CHAPTER 25

FLORENCE HAD JUST FINISHED FEEDING her baby and was burping her over her shoulder when Carter rushed down the stairs. "Wilma's coming."

Florence froze and it was a moment before she could talk. "She's coming here?"

"Yes. She's walking up to the house."

Florence sat down on the couch, still holding the baby against her. "What is this about?" She'd given up hoping her stepmother would come around and want to see the baby. Still, she'd prayed, and she knew that God could perform miracles.

Carter was by her side in a flash. "Shall I answer the door?"

She stared at Carter's nervous face.

As much as he said he didn't care that his birth mother didn't accept him, he had to be hoping that she would. He had no brothers or sisters, and with his birth father and his adoptive mother both gone it was natural for him to want some contact with Wilma. "I think you should."

Florence didn't say it, but she hoped that Wilma wasn't there to complain about something. She could've been there to complain about Cherish's farm, or something that they might have said to Cherish in the car on the way back. Anything was possible. Wilma hadn't been a happy woman since her first husband, Florence's father, died. And according to the girls, that hadn't changed when she married Levi.

She watched the anticipation on her husband's face. He'd been upset by Wilma but not as many times as she had. She didn't want to see him suffer through it one more time.

When he had his hand on the doorhandle, Florence got up with the baby still in her arms and stood behind Carter.

When he opened the door, Wilma was walking up the porch steps, smiling.

She looked like the old Wilma, the woman who'd raised her.

"Hello Carter, and Florence."

"Hello, Wilma," Carter said with a touch of ice in his voice.

"Nice to see you, Wilma."

"I know things haven't been good with us in the past. And I do have myself to blame for that. I'm sorry if I hurt you, Carter and you are probably upset with me too, Florence."

Relief washed over Florence. She was here in peace. And probably to see the baby.

Carter said, "Would you like to come in and hold your granddaughter?"

Tears came to Wilma's eyes. "I would like that very much."

"Here she is," said Florence. "Let's sit on the couch, Wilma." It didn't feel right to call her *Mamm* anymore. There was a divide between them since Florence had left the community, and that was something that couldn't be changed.

Florence passed the baby over. Wilma held the tightly wrapped baby in the crook of her elbow. "Ah, she's beautiful. She looks a lot like Mercy. And a little bit like Cherish."

"What are Mercy and Honor's babies like?"

"Big *bopplis*. Big *bu bopplis*. This is my first grand-daughter and she'll always have a special place in my heart." She looked up at Florence. "And so will you, Florence. You were my first real *dochder*."

Tears came to Florence's eyes and she couldn't hold them back. A tear trickled down her face and Carter got up and passed her a tissue.

In the past, Wilma had always referred to her as her stepdaughter and always corrected people when they said she was Wilma's daughter.

Florence had thought she was past caring about

Wilma, but she wasn't. It meant everything to hear that. Wilma, with all her faults was the only mother Florence had ever known.

"That's nice to hear, Wilma. Thank you."

Wilma smiled at her and then looked at Carter. "I know you think I gave you away and didn't care."

"That's what you told me, Wilma, so that's what I thought."

Wilma's bottom lip wobbled, and her mouth opened to speak and then she hesitated a moment. "I spoke in anger. What mother doesn't think about a child she's given birth to?"

Florence stared at her sleeping baby. "I can't imagine that a day wouldn't go by that you didn't think of that little baby boy."

"I gave you the biggest, best gift I could—my sister. She gave you a life that I could never give you. I wouldn't have been accepted in the community. I would've traveled a hard road and … I was scared."

Then Florence remembered Wilma saying she'd closed the door on her sister when she needed her. Was that after Wilma had given Iris her baby? Whatever faults Wilma had and no matter what she'd done, she was here now. It took a lot for her to admit she was scared as a young unmarried and pregnant Amish woman. Florence held her breath waiting for Carter to speak.

"You made a good decision, Wilma. For yourself,

and for me. I can't imagine not having Iris as my mother. She was the best."

"I know. I knew she would've been. Can you forgive me for turning my back?"

"We can," Carter said.

It was just the same as in Florence's dream of a few months before. She'd had a dream that Wilma came to the door and asked their forgiveness. The only difference was Wilma had been dressed in her Sunday best wearing a pretty light blue dress.

"Florence, I wasn't nice to you when you left. I know there is a rift that divides us with you now being on the outside, but I want you to know you will always have a fond place in my heart." She looked down at the baby in her arms. "What is this little one's name?"

Carter and Florence looked at one another. "We haven't decided yet."

"We do have a last name," Carter joked.

"Did you get the blanket I made for her?"

"We did, and it's so beautiful. Thank you. She has it over her all the time. I asked the girls to thank you. I'm not sure if they did. I know they can be forgetful."

"I'm pleased you found a use for it." Wilma leaned down and kissed the baby on her forehead. "I should get back. I've left Hope in charge of the cooking and that dreadful rabbit has been found and brought back to the house."

"Bliss will be pleased about that."

"And, the boy from the orchard next door is joining us."

"Fairfax?"

"Yes. That's the one. I heard it from someone who heard it from someone else. He had a meeting with our bishop."

Florence laughed. "Some things never change. There can never be any secrets in the community."

Wilma smiled. "Looks like Hope is fond of him if I'm not wrong. He must like her too, since he's joining our community. We might have another wedding next year." Wilma passed the baby back to Florence and then stood.

Both Florence and Carter walked her to the door. When she got there, she turned around and offered another rare smile. Then before another awkward moment was had, she turned and walked down the two porch steps.

Carter put his arm around Florence's shoulder as they watched her leave.

WHEN WILMA WAS HALFWAY to the orchard, Florence said, "I had a dream that she apologized, and it happened."

"I remember that day. Amazing."

"That's the Wilma who raised me."

"I hope we get to see more of her."

"Me too."

When she had passed out of sight, Carter closed the door. "What do you think about Fairfax becoming Amish and possibly marrying one of your bonnet sisters?"

"That was a shock. I can hardly believe it. Hope must be so happy."

"I could tell he was in love with one of them."

Florence laughed. "I keep telling you not to call them the bonnet sisters."

He took Florence by the arm and took her and the baby back to the couch. "Forget your sisters. What we have to figure out is what to call this little girl."

Florence looked down at her. "I know we do."

THE NEXT MORNING in the Baker household, Bliss's frantic screams rang out through the silent, still house. Cherish was first in the room expecting to see her half dead, attacked by some intruder. When she saw Bliss leaning over the hutch, she thought Bruiser was dead.

She ran to comfort Bliss, then she saw what Bliss was looking at. Four baby balls of fur were beside Bruiser. "Where did they come from?" asked Cherish.

"Bruiser had babies."

"That's impossible. He's a boy." Cherish gasped. She'd been tricked. "That's what I was told."

Bliss threw her arms around her. *"Denke,* Cherish. I'm glad Bruisers a girl."

Then everyone else arrived to see what the commotion was.

"Dat, I'm a *grossmammi,"* Bliss said to her father.

He chuckled.

"We're not keeping them," said Wilma crossing her arms over her chest. "You can get rid of them as soon as they're old enough."

"Ach, Mamm. Can't we keep them all?"

"Nee, Bliss." *Mamm* turned and stomped away, and Levi went with her.

All the girls stared at the baby rabbits.

"I can't believe Adam told me Bruiser was a boy. He must've known he wasn't a boy. I don't think I would've bought him had I known."

"It's okay, Cherish. I'm glad he's a girl. I'll just have to change his name. Bruiser isn't a nice name for a girl. I'll call her … Marshmallow, because her tail looks like a marshmallow."

Cherish wasn't listening to her. All she could think about was giving Adam a piece of her mind. How dare he say he didn't want to see her because she wasn't rabbit-worthy, and all the while he was lying about Bruiser being a girl. "If I ever see that man I bought Bruiser from again, I'm telling him exactly what I think of him." Cherish growled and her hands curled into fists. He must've known.

"*Nee,* don't, Cherish. I love, Bruiser. I mean, Marshmallow. I knew he was getting fat, I just didn't know why."

Favor and Hope giggled, and then Bliss joined them. Cherish could barely suppress the smile that tugged at her lips. When the girls kept laughing, Cherish finally saw the funny side of everything and couldn't help laughing along with them.

Thank you for reading A Baby For Florence. I hope you are enjoying the series.
So you don't miss out on any of my new releases and special offers, be sure to add your email on the newsletter section of my website.
www.SamanthaPriceAuthor.com
Blessings,
Samantha Price

The next in the series is Book #10
Amish Bliss

AN ANGRY LETTER from Cherish brings a young man back into town to deliver an apology in person. How does Cherish feel when she sees him again?

Hope is delighted when the man she loves joins her Amish community so they can eventually marry. Will the isolation from the outside world prove too much for him?

What happens when Wilma and her new husband leave the girls alone for a quick vacation? Will there even be a house standing on their return?

Meanwhile, Bliss finds someone with whom she has

a lot in common. Cherish tells Bliss he's hiding something, but is he?

You will love this sweet and wholesome Amish romance series because there is never a dull moment in the bonnet sisters' world.

Grab your copy now and get caught up with volume ten of their story. Amish Bliss

THE AMISH BONNET SISTERS

Book 1 Amish Mercy

Book 2 Amish Honor

Book 3 A Simple Kiss

Book 4 Amish Joy

Book 5 Amish Family Secrets

Book 6 The Englisher

Book 7 Missing Florence

Book 8 Their Amish Stepfather

Book 9 A Baby For Florence

Book 10 Amish Bliss

ABOUT SAMANTHA PRICE

USA Today Bestselling author, Samantha Price, wrote stories from a young age, but it wasn't until later in life that she took up writing full time. Formally an artist, she exchanged her paintbrush for the computer and, many best-selling book series later, has never looked back.

Samantha is happiest on her computer lost in the world of her characters. She is best known for the Ettie Smith Amish Mysteries series and the Expectant Amish Widows series.

www.SamanthaPriceAuthor.com

Samantha loves to hear from her readers. Connect with her at:

samantha@samanthapriceauthor.com
www.facebook.com/SamanthaPriceAuthor
Follow Samantha Price on BookBub
Twitter @ AmishRomance
Instagram - SamanthaPriceAuthor